Matchless

Leslie DuBois

Matchless

Leslie DuBois

LITTLE
PRINCE
PUBLISHING

Leslie DuBois

Matchless Copyright © 2019 Leslie DuBois

Published by Little Prince Publishing in Charleston, South Carolina.
Cover Design: Jessica Richardson

ISBN-13: 978-1-939947-10-9
ISBN-10: 1-939947-10-3

Printed in the United States of America
Visit www.LittlePrincePublishing.com

Leslie DuBois

Chapter 1: Xander

It was April 8th, our six-month anniversary, when it happened. I know six months doesn't seem like a very long time. And technically, it's not really an anniversary until a year but we were high school kids. Six months is a really long time for a high school relationship. It meant we were serious. So serious that I wanted to tell Bria Browning how I really felt about her. I wanted to tell her I loved her.

I had planned the perfect day. We had just finished skating on the lake behind my house under a gentle snowfall. I was wearing the hat that she had knitted for me and given me that morning. It was a dark blue color that she said matched my eyes perfectly. I didn't know when she had time to knit between making straight As, being the president of nearly every club at school and tagging along with me to my practices. But Bria was always able to do anything she set her mind to. And I do mean anything. All she needed was a little research and nothing was impossible for her to accomplish.

I remember it was a Wednesday because that was the night my mother had book club so she wasn't home. She never missed book club ever. My dad was at an away game with the Colorado Avalanche and my sister Kimmy was at the rink. We had the house to ourselves when I brought Bria to my basement. The house was always empty whenever I brought Bria over. I wasn't sure why, but subconsciously I knew that I shouldn't tell my parents that I was dating a black girl.

It was in my basement that I gave her my latest gift. A puzzle. Not just any puzzle. I had found an impossible, abstract, never-ending jigsaw puzzle. She loved puzzles and I loved watching her figure them out. The way her brain worked was pure art. I pretended to help, but really I just sat back and watched while sipping hot cocoa.

"Why are you staring at me like that?" she asked suddenly.

"Like what?" I asked, scooting closer to her.

"Like that."

Instead of answering her, I leaned in and kissed her. Her lips tasted like warm peppermint cocoa. Bria Browning wasn't my first kiss but she was definitely my best. A lot of girls kissed like it was a race to get to the next thing. But Bria kissed me as if the kiss itself were the finish line, the culmination of our feelings.

Now it was time to tell her. Time to say those words I had felt since before she had even agreed to go out with me six months ago.

I pulled away from her so slightly that our lips were still practically touching. That was when she said, "I love you, Xander."

Damn it. She said it first. I was just about to say it as well when my dad burst into the basement and yelled, "What the hell is going on in here?"

"Dad," I said, hopping up. I didn't know why at the time but I felt the need to put distance between Bria and myself. "I thought you were in Toronto."

"Answer the question, Alexander," he said through gritted teeth.

"Dad, this is Bria Brow ... "

"I know who she is and she needs to get out of my house. Now!"

Well, that was the nice version of what he said as he turned around and punched a hole in the wall. Before my father could finish his racist, profanity-laden tirade, I had whisked Bria outside and into my car.

We were both too shocked to say anything on the way back to her house. And even when we pulled into her driveway ten minutes later, we still couldn't speak. I guessed we were trying to process what had just happened. What must she think of me if my father could just call her those vile names?

"I'm sorry," I said finally. "I really don't know what that was about."

She remained silent and wouldn't look at me. She just kept staring straight ahead. *Look at me please. I love you. I don't care what he says*, I said in my head. Why didn't I say it out loud? What was wrong with me?

"I'll call you tomorrow, okay?" I said.

"Please don't," she said before fleeing my car.

I returned to my house determined to confront my father about the way he had treated the woman I loved. I usually stayed away from Patrick Vaughn as much as possible. His quick, violent temper was so encouraged during a hockey game that sometimes he had a hard time turning it off when he was home. I should have backed off a little when I saw him drinking whiskey straight from the bottle, but I was too angry. I don't remember what I said, but I do remember flying through the air and landing on the kitchen table, collapsing it into several pieces.

"God damn it, Patrick, he has Regionals in two weeks," my mother said.

Regionals? Really? My father had just thrown me across the room and she was concerned about me being in peak physical condition for a figure skating competition?

"This is your fault," he said to her. "Tell him. Tell him why he can't see the Browning kid."

"I didn't know they were together," my mother said. But that was a lie. Why was she lying to my father?

"Tell him. Tell him why he can't see her," he said.

My mother sighed and looked at me as if all of this were my fault. "I told you this wasn't a good idea," she said in Russian. She always spoke Russian when she didn't want my father to understand. "Now that he's seen you together, you absolutely cannot be with her anymore. It will destroy this family," she added matter-of-factly. Helping me to my feet, she said, "Go take an ibuprofen and sit in an ice bath. You need to be ready for rink time in the morning. I'll handle your father."

And that was it. The last time we ever spoke about Bria Browning. And the last time I called Patrick Vaughn my father.

Chapter 2: Bria

I didn't care about racism. I really didn't. It probably sounded inauthentic coming from an impressionable black teenage girl. Most teenage girls were insecure and completely obsessed with what other people thought of them. I was not saying I didn't have my insecurities. Everyone did. But my skin color wasn't one of them.

The truth was, I'd thought about it long and hard and I really didn't care about racism mostly due to my Snow Boot Theory. See, in my estimation, racism was dumber than hating someone because of their snow boots.

Let's say someone was wearing a pair of snow boots that I despised. They were ugly, they didn't match anything, they leaked and they tracked snow into my house or whatever. They were just not good boots for whatever reason. I hated the stupid snow boots and the person wearing them. But they could change their snow boots quite easily actually, so it was stupid to hate them over it.

Let's extrapolate that to hating someone over their skin color. Well, that was something they couldn't change no matter how hard they tried. They had no control over their skin color. Therefore, it made more sense to hate someone over their snow boots, which they could change, than to hate them over their skin color, which they could not. And why would I hate someone over snow boots? That would make me an idiot. Voila! The Snow Boot Theory.

Racism made the racist stupid, not me. I was fine with Patrick Vaughn hating me because of my skin color. I never thought he was too bright in the first place. Too many hockey pucks to the face if you asked me. I was not worried about Patrick Vaughn. I was worried about my Xander. How would his father's reaction to me affect him? He was probably really hurting right now, perhaps even physically if he got into another fight with his father. I didn't want to be the cause of any pain in his life. On the other hand, if he felt for me half of what I felt for him, it would be too painful for me not to be in his life. I had a tough decision to make. I stared at my phone, wanting him to call and not call at the same time.

After two hours of staring at my phone, I shrieked in frustration. What was I doing? I was the one who told him not to call! I threw my phone across the room then I took out a sheet of paper and started writing out Pascal's triangle. It was a simple mathematical escape to help me forget all that I was feeling. I hated feeling this much; it was ridiculous and illogical but I couldn't help it. I loved that boy with everything in me. When I was with him, I felt feelings I didn't know existed. His piercing blue eyes and thick, black hair haunted my dreams and my waking hours. There wasn't a minute of the day when he wasn't somewhere in my thoughts. And one of my foremost thoughts was what in the world did he see in me?

The beautiful, talented Alexander Dmitri Vaughn, who was on track to make the Olympic figure skating team, wanted *me* of all people. Me, a borderline freak of nature. I could do nothing for him. Nothing but bring him down. Maybe it would be best if we were apart.

~~~

While I didn't care at all what people thought of me, Xander cared too much. Which was probably why he found himself in a particularly bad situation one Saturday night two months after we had broken up.

I got a mysterious phone call at 2 a.m. Normally, I wouldn't answer a random phone number in the middle of the night, but I had to admit, I was curious. No one ever called me.

"Bria, are you busy?" an obviously inebriated voice said over the phone.

"Kimmy?" I asked. It was Xander's sister. We were pretty good friends while Xander and I were together, but not call each other randomly at 2 a.m. kind of friends. I knew something was up.

"How did you know?" she asked exuberantly.

"Are you drunk?"

"Yes, I am super drunk, but we have bigger problems, Bria. Stop trying to distract me."

"What's going on?" I was starting to get nervous. What could possibly be a bigger problem than Kimmy being drunk? The Vaughns would kill her if they found out. Oh, no. Xander. "Kimmy, where is your brother?" I asked.

"He's right here," she sang.

"Let me speak to him."

"No can do, Bria-roo. He's, like, not talking."

"Kimmy, why is he not talking? Where are you two?" I asked while simultaneously putting my shoes on.

"Xander is taking a little nap on the bathroom floor."

"Did he go to sleep or did he pass out?" I asked. There was no response.

"Kimmy? Kimmy, are you there?"

"I'm heeeeeere," she sang again.

"Kimmy, is Xander breathing?" I spoke slowly and clearly to make sure she understood me.

"I'm not a doctor. How am I supposed to know that?"

I sighed. This was going nowhere. I had to find them and figure this out myself. But Kimmy was in no position to give me directions to where they were and I couldn't feasibly drive all over the city of Denver until I found them.

"Okay, Kimmy, I am texting you a link to a locator app. Just click on the link, then hit accept and I will be able to find you."

Kimmy and Xander turned out to be at a pool party thrown by rising senior Mitchell Clark. After checking three bathrooms, I found them in the bathroom of the pool house. Xander was pale, almost naked and sprawled out on the floor, while Kimmy was curled up next to the toilet, scrolling through pictures on her phone. She looked dazed and almost ready to pass out herself. I was just happy she called me in time.

"What happened?"

"He's drunk. And he won't wake up. And we need to go home because it's way past curfew. And I don't have my license yet. We have to get home before he realizes we are gone. If Dad finds out we've been drinking, he is going to take away skating. Definitely no skating for us. We have to skate. We're going to the Olympics, you know?"

I checked Xander's pulse. It was so faint I had to force myself not to panic. "How much did he drink?"

"I am going to win a gold medal while wearing a pale blue sequined jumpsuit to match my eyes. I don't know what Xander is gonna wear. He hates sequins for some silly reason. But the more sparkle the better if you ask me. Or you can ask Beyoncé."

"Kimmy, focus. How much did he drink?"

"How am I supposed to know that? And to go with the pale blue sequined jumpsuit I'm gonna straighten my curly hair so that it's finally straight. Straight like Xander's. You know when my hair is straight, it reaches my waist!"

"How did this happen? This boy drinks kale and wheat germ smoothies every day," I said, tending to Xander while ignoring Kimmy's ramblings. "He doesn't even drink soda. The most unhealthy thing he puts in his body is organic hot cocoa. Since when does he drink—"

"Vodka," Kimmy said, interrupting me. "Lots and lots of vodka."

"Since when does he drink vodka?" I asked.

"Since you two broke up," she said before going into more descriptions of skating costumes.

I felt my chest tighten. He was in pain. He had needed me and I hadn't been there for him.

"We have to get him to a hospital," I said, rolling him onto his side.

"Nope. No hospital," Kimmy said, looking at her phone. "I may be a little drunk." She paused and looked at me. "Okay, I'm a lot drunk. But I'm not stupid. If we show up at the hospital like this we can kiss skating goodbye."

"And if you're dead, you will also never skate again."

Sobering up slightly, she said, "You think he could die?"

"Kimmy, his pulse is so low I barely feel it. I have no idea how much he drank. He's unrespons—" Just then, Xander started vomiting.

"Help me get him up," I said to Kimmy. After we got him positioned over the toilet, most of the vomit made it in. He kept coughing and vomiting for a good five minutes when finally, he started moaning.

"It's okay, Xander. You're going to be okay," I said, stroking his hair. I found a towel and cleaned him up while still forcing myself to stay calm. The vomiting made me feel better actually. He was getting some of the poison out of him. And since he was moaning, he was at least responsive. Maybe I would delay the hospital.

Somehow, Kimmy and I were able to get him into my car. When we got to the Vaughn house, we didn't even attempt to get him upstairs. Instead, we took him to the home gym and dressed him in workout clothes. Since it was almost time for him to start his morning workout, it wouldn't look weird that he was in there if his parents happened to peek in.

After getting him on the couch, he looked up at me and said, "Bria Bear, is that you?"

I ran my fingers through his thick black hair and kissed his forehead. Even though he was completely gross and smelly, I still wanted to wrap my arms around him and hold him. "It's me, Xanadu" I said. That was our thing. He thought I looked like a teddy bear the first time we met with my hair in curly puffs. His name and the fact that he skated reminded me of that horrible Olivia Newton-John movie Xanadu. So those became our pet names for each other. "You've had a lot to drink. You're not going to remember any of this in the morning."

"My Bria Bear," he whispered before falling asleep again. I checked his pulse and his breathing. He really was going to be fine. He'd have a terrible headache in the morning, but I no longer felt a hospital was necessary. But since I wasn't a doctor, I wasn't confident enough in my diagnosis to leave him. I spent the rest of the night right by his side, checking his pulse and monitoring his breathing.

Three hours later, I heard someone come down the stairs. The steps were too heavy to be Kimmy so I just assumed it was Patrick Vaughn. I hid behind the couch just in case he poked his head in the gym. I didn't want a repeat of what happened on our sixth month anniversary.

Patrick Vaughn stepped into the gym and stared at his son on the couch. If he had stepped in any further, he definitely would have seen me. Instead, he just said, "Typical. Can't even finish a workout," before heading out the door. Thankfully, I had thought in advance to park down the street so my car wasn't in their driveway.

"You're still here?" Kimmy said to me an hour later while sipping a cup of coffee.

"Yeah." I stood up from my uncomfortable position on the floor and stretched. "I wanted to make sure he was okay. He's been talking in his sleep so I think he's fine."

"What's he saying?" she asked.

I shrugged. "Mostly skating terms, I guess."

There was a pause in which Kimmy stared down at her feet for a moment. Finally, she said, "Look, Bria, I really want to thank you for last night. You didn't have to help us. But you really ... probably literally saved our lives. And I'm sure Xan will be super appreciative as well."

"You cannot tell him I was here!" I said.

"What? Why?" she asked, obviously surprised at my firm tone.

I shook my head. "Do you know how embarrassed he would be if he knew the girl he dumped saw him like this? No, he can never know. Save him a little dignity."

"But ... but what am I supposed to tell him?"

"I don't care what you tell him, but you have to promise me that you will not tell him that he puked on his ex-girlfriend while in his underwear."

"Um ... "

"Promise me, Kimmy."

"Okay, I promise."

Chapter 3: Xander

High school was so weird. Bria had a theory that high school was like a different planet and high school students like aliens. It made sense to me. There was an ecosystem, a food chain—a hierarchy that made absolutely no logical sense and had to be set in place by aliens. That was the only explanation for how a girl like Heidi Hopley could rise to high school royalty for absolutely no reason at all. She wasn't smart, she wasn't that pretty in my opinion, and she wasn't even a cheerleader or anything. I thought that was the stereotype. The cheerleaders were the popular girls. But on planet Cherry Hill High, the cheerleaders, and the dance team, and every girl on campus looked to Heidi for what was cool. It was bizarre. She was the Kim Kardashian of Cherry Hill.

On the odd, alien planet of high school, survival was the name of the game. And as long as you kept your head down and stayed in your lane, you could survive for the most part. Sometimes something happened and you could hop on an elevator to the top of the food chain. Other times you got tripped and got pushed onto the highway to high school hell.

Right after Bria and I broke up, I caught the elevator. I had already started working out so my body had finally grown to fit my giant head. Suddenly, I was a hottie. Also, Kimmy and I started getting more and more news coverage for figure skating so I became a pseudo popular kid. I say pseudo because I was never really one of them. I didn't have time to play school sports, go for pizza after school or perpetually get drunk on weekends. But figure skating and a couple of parties was enough to make me Heidi-approved.

Bria, on the other hand, took the brunt of our failed relationship during our junior year. Before we were together, she was just ignored. But something about the way I talked about her or looked at her or something put her on Heidi's radar. And once that happened she was determined to keep Bria in her place.

~~~

Bria usually ate lunch in the school newspaper office in order to avoid drama from people like Heidi. But one day during the first week of senior year, she had shown up in the cafeteria. I think I was so shocked that I was probably staring, which gave Heidi the motivation to do what she did next.

"Oh my God, Brian," she said loudly. "What the hell are you wearing?" At this point a hush had fallen over the cafeteria. That usually happened whenever Heidi spoke. Everyone wanted to hear what stupidity would fall out of her mouth. It didn't skip my attention that she called Bria "Brian." It was one of her favorite tactics, trying to claim Bria looked like a man or something. Which was ridiculous by the way. Bria was stunningly beautiful in an adorable way. I always thought she could have her own TV show on the Disney Channel or something.

Bria looked down at herself and responded, "They're called clothes," in her classic matter-of-fact voice. A few people giggled, thinking that Bria had just leveled a diss at Heidi. But I knew that Bria was just stating the obvious.

Heidi was pissed at the perceived joke at her expense and continued her attack. "Clothes? I don't think so. More like trash. You look like a homeless reject from a Star Trek convention."

Wow, that was the dumbest insult I had ever heard. There was nothing Star Trek about what Bria was wearing. She wore white knee socks, a blue pleated skirt and white button down shirt. As always, she accessorized with a mini backpack and a matching pair of Beats headphones. It was Wednesday so that meant red. If I ever wanted to know what day of the week it was all I had to do was check to see what color headphones and backpack Bria Browning was wearing. Mondays, purple. Tuesdays, blue. Wednesdays, red. Thursdays, green. Fridays, white and weekends were black.

Anyway, with the blue pleated skirt and white shirt, there was more of a Sailor Moon vibe that was equal parts retro and adorable as usual. Star Trek was probably the only nerdy thing Heidi could think of, so she went with it. Stupid as it was, somehow it was enough to get cheers from her idiot followers.

Bria stared at Heidi for an awkwardly long time while Heidi threw out some other ridiculous insults. Bria just stood there and took it while everyone laughed at her. I felt so bad for her. I felt I had to do something to come to her defense. I wanted to use my popularity to help her. Turns out I didn't have to.

"4178-6593-3883-9301," Bria yelled. By the time she was finished saying her long string of numbers, the cafeteria had grown quiet again.

"What the hell was that?" Heidi asked.

"Your credit card number," Bria said. "I got a glimpse of it when you paid for your yearbook this morning and I have a photographic memory. Did you catch that?" Bria asked, looking around. "Everyone, get your phone out and fill up your Amazon cart. It's on Heidi. I'll start again. 4178—"

"Shut up!" Heidi yelled in panicked frustration.

"Listen, Heidi," Bria said calmly. "Leave me alone or I will ruin you. I'm smart enough to do it." Bria cracked open her soda, took a sip then walked out of the cafeteria like a boss.

Damn, I loved that girl.

~~~

I tried to get over Bria. I really, really did. I had a string of girlfriends from my high school and even neighboring ones. I even dated Heidi for a hot second. And I do mean a second. Once she figured out that I didn't have time to be her arm candy on weekends, I was tossed aside.

It didn't matter. No girl could ever come close to what Bria meant to me. None of them listened to me like she did or attempted to learn Russian for me. None of them were able to make the world make sense with just one seemingly out of touch analogy that actually made everything click into place. None of them kissed me like she did. None of them not only didn't mind hanging out at the skating rink in order to spend time with me but actually preferred it. Most other girls made me feel guilty for all the time I had to spend skating. In summary, there was only one Bria Browning and she currently hated me.

After several months of trying to find a replacement Bria, I settled into something different. I called it "Operation BB Hate." I realized that even though she justifiably hated me with every fiber of her being, I didn't hate her. I still loved her. I had to manufacture ways to see her. Unfortunately, "Operation BB Hate" involved me lying to everyone in my family.

During one of my BB Hate missions, my little sister Kimmy showed up at my school and almost wrecked it.

"What are you doing here?" I asked her. She was only two years younger than me so she should have been in school with me but she opted to homeschool in order to have more time to train. Kimmy would literally skate twenty-four hours a day if she could. I usually had to remind her to sleep and eat.

She shrugged. "What are you still doing here? You've been staying after school a lot," she said, taking a drink from a can.

"Kimmy, what the hell are you drinking?"

She looked at the can and then looked at me like I was an idiot. "It's called Red Bull. It's an energy drink."

"Those things are disgusting. They're like rocket fuel. It's straight up poison."

"I remember a time when you used to drink poison," she said. I knew she was referring to the first few weeks after Bria dumped me. I didn't take it too well and resorted to drinking. A lot. But when I woke up one morning after a night of drinking in my workout room with a horrible headache and no clue of how I had gotten there, I stopped and went back to my usual healthy habits.

"That's cold, Kimmy," I said, reeling from her insensitive remark.

"You're right. I'm sorry, Xan." She closed her eyes and took a deep breath. "I'm just so tired. I needed a pick-me-up."

"If you're tired, take a nap. Don't drink that garbage."

Kimmy sighed. "I've been sleeping all day, now I need to make up some rink time and I want you to come with me."

I glanced at my phone. This was the worst timing ever.

"Well, if you missed your rink time then you can make it up by yourself," I said, going on the offensive slightly.

"Well, Renitsky has a new jump sequence he wants us to try. You need to come on."

"I thought you said you just wanted to make up rink time. Now you're bringing in Coach. What's going on?"

"Why can't it be both?" she asked.

I hated having to doubt my little sister. I just knew too well my parents' tendency to spy on me. And this felt like an ambush.

"I can't today. I'm busy," I said.

"You're not busy," she said dismissively. "You have skating and school. That's it. School is over so let's go skate."

"I have someplace to be, Kimmy. I have a life. I have friends. I have other things to do besides skating."

Kimmy stared at me. I tried to meet her gaze, but I turned away after a few seconds. My little sister had a way of seeing straight through me.

"You might as well tell me now where you're going 'cause I'm not leaving till you do," she said before taking another swig of that poison in a can.

"I'm not telling you so go away."

"Is it a new girlfriend? It better not be that redhead from the concession stand at the rink. She better not be feeding you ice cream and pizza. You're in training; you can't eat that trash."

"You're one to talk," I said, gesturing to the can. "I don't have a girlfriend and I'm not eating junk food, okay?"

But she wasn't okay. She wouldn't let it go which meant she definitely wasn't just asking for herself. She was definitely spying for mom and maybe even Patrick.

"Fine," I said after she stared at me long enough. "I'm going to a chess tournament."

Raising an eyebrow she said, "Since when do you play chess?"

"I don't. I'm not going to play. I'm going to watch."

She rolled her eyes. "You expect me to believe you're going to watch a chess match?"

"Not just a match. It's a tournament. That's more than one match."

"Oh my sweet Cheez-Its! Bria is on the chess team, isn't she?"

I didn't respond.

"Please don't tell me you're going to a chess tournament just to get a glimpse of your ex-girlfriend. Xan, that is pathetic."

"It's not pathetic. I find chess interesting and Bria happens to be the best at it."

Kimmy stared at me unconvinced.

"She really is the best. I think she can see, like, eight moves ahead and predict what her opponent is going to do. She does the cutest thing with her lips when she sees a way to win. She'll, like, purse her lips together and push them to the right. When she does that, she is gonna win in, like, eight moves or less."

Kimmy kept staring.

"But if she rolls her lips in until they practically disappear, then she's in trouble. But she usually gets out of it somehow. It really is amazing. I mean, I barely understand what each piece does and she can somehow just see the whole board and all the possibilities."

"I can't even with you right now," Kimmy said, rolling her eyes. She tossed her can into the garbage can next to my bench and then gathered her long, curly black hair into a ponytail. "Do you hear yourself? Just tell her how you feel and get back together with her."

"I can't do that and you know why."

Kimmy sighed.

"Please don't tell them," I begged. She knew I was referring to our parents.

"Fine, I'll cover for you ... again. But you owe me."

"Whatever you want. I'm good for it."

"I want whatever cash is in your wallet right now," she said, holding out her hand. "I want the purple sequined costume for Nationals and I want you not to tell Mom about my being, like, extra tired lately."

I opened my wallet. "Here's a twenty and I won't tell Mom about your new rocket fuel addiction, but the purple sequins is out, Kimmy. I'm serious."

"Deal," she said, taking the twenty. "But I'm telling our parents you have explosive diarrhea and you need to be close to a toilet for the next three hours. Trust me, it is less embarrassing than creeping on your ex at a chess match."

I shrugged. "That's fair."

Chapter 4: Bria

He broke my heart into a thousand pieces like a sledgehammer to glass and I should have hated him. But instead, the worst I could bring myself to do was miss him.

There was an emptiness inside me that pulled me out of sleep's grasp every morning at 4 a.m. That was the time he started lifting weights in his home gym. When we were together, he used to send me a text that said "Good Morning, Beautiful" every day at that time. He thought my phone would be on Do Not Disturb so it wouldn't wake me, but the truth was I loved being woken up by that text. He had sent that wake up text to me 182 times and I cherished each one. They showed that I was the first thing on his mind every morning and that he thought I was ... beautiful.

After lifting weights for an hour, he would shower, grab a protein drink, and then head to the rink with his sister. At the same time, that emptiness inside me forced me to shower, then to get dressed and then to shovel the thick, endless Denver snow off of my car so that I could drive thirty minutes to sit in the shadows and get a glimpse of him skating. It's weird, it's sick and not to mention possibly illegal, but I couldn't stop.

When he first dumped me, I tried to completely cut him out of my life. We never had any classes together at school so I didn't have to worry about that but after dating for six months, we had our secret meet ups. Xander had a particularly boring and unobservant history teacher during third period, which was the same time I had newspaper. We would both sneak out of class and meet in the art department hallway by the broken vending machines. Now I couldn't walk by any vending machine without thinking of making out with him. I avoided that hallway like it was a telemarketer with the plague. I also had to park in a different parking lot to avoid seeing him in the mornings. And God forbid I went to the cafeteria and saw him eating lunch with Horrible Heidi Hopley again.

I was very successful at avoiding all possible contact with Xander for the remainder of our junior year. But once summer started, I was so profoundly lonely I was desperate to see him. I held out pretty well until that night Kimmy called me for help. After sitting next to him all night, hearing his breathing, running my fingers through his hair, I couldn't stay away any longer. I started going to his skating rink once in a while and that turned into every day.

Xander skated twice a day every day except Sunday, but I could only watch him during his morning workout. That was when there was peace and no one around to ask me what on earth I was doing there. After stalking him for six months straight, I had somehow convinced myself that it was okay and it was not hurting anyone and it was in fact keeping me sane.

My parents hadn't even noticed. Or maybe they did notice and they just didn't care. In any case, every day I waited for them to somehow acknowledge my existence. I wanted them to wonder why I was leaving the house almost three hours before school started every day.

Today was actually no different. My dad was in his study pouring over patient files. I slammed down a coffee mug against the counter, hoping to get his attention. It worked ... Kinda.

"Annette, did you make coffee?" he yelled through the door.

"Mom is still in New York shopping. I made coffee though," I said, then added under my breath, "Just like I do every morning. It's on a freaking timer."

I dutifully poured a cup and brought it to him. After setting it on his desk, I hesitated a moment, silently praying that he would ask where I was going so early in the morning or how my classes were or if I had all my college applications in or something. Anything! But he didn't even look up from his paperwork. I stared at his too-good-to-be-true looks. It sucked being the child of two amazingly gorgeous people. My father was of mixed race and therefore had this light almond skin along with these glowing, pale blue eyes. My mother, with her smooth, rich, dark skin, actually did some modeling in her younger days. Unfortunately, I didn't take after them in the looks department. I was short and frumpy with big, frizzy hair.

My dad took a sip of coffee, then another, and another. Finally, he looked up and said, "It's good. Thanks."

As I drove to the rink that morning, I told myself it was nothing to get upset about. I mean, most teenagers would love to have parents that gave them complete, free reign. I was eighteen years old and I'd never had a curfew, I'd had my own credit card since I was twelve, and my parents had never once asked me to call them and check in. I tried to tell myself that it was only because I had never been in trouble and my parents trusted me immensely. It was better than the alternative, right? Xander's parents were basically the Gestapo compared to my parents. They constantly had to know where he was going, what he was doing, who it was with and when he'd be back. The same for Kimmy. And because they were such elite athletes, their parents even controlled what they ate sometimes. About a year and a half ago, the summer right before Xander and I got together, the Vaughns made Kimmy start a food diary when they thought she was gaining too much weight. This was a bit too far for Xander, however. He started lifting weights and bulking up so he'd be able to lift his sister during their routines no matter what she weighed. That was the kind of guy Xander was. He was so caring, warm, and loving. He looked for ways to make other people happy. Other people who weren't me, I guessed.

Parking my car at the Cherry Hill Ice Rink, I sighed. Deep down I knew Xander didn't mean to hurt me. I remember when he promised he would never hurt me. He would want to make me happy if he could. But he couldn't, obviously. I was sure his parents threatened to take away skating if he continued seeing me. That would be the real crime. I would never forgive myself if I got in the way of his skating career.

I was a few minutes late that morning so Kimmy and Xander had already started their Nationals' routine when I walked in. I could hear the music to "From Eden" by Hozier. I took my usual spot in the top part of the stands where no one could see me and I stared at my Alexander Dmitri Vaughn. He was pure joy and beauty in motion. Watching him left me breathless. Kimmy was good too, but Xander ... He had that indescribable quality that made it impossible for anyone to take their eyes off of him. Depriving the world of his talent would be a flat-out sin. I couldn't let that happen, especially when they were so close to their dream of qualifying for the Olympics.

Most figure skaters who trained as much as Xander and Kimmy would homeschool in order to have more ice time. Kimmy homeschooled but not Xander, though. School was his only chance to get away from his parents. That meant two hours of ice time before school each day and another three hours each evening. Honestly, I didn't know how he did it. Most days I needed a nap after just watching him for an hour or so.

After Xander's workout on the ice came my absolute favorite part of the morning. He would step off the ice and simultaneously whip off his shirt. His perfectly sculpted physique made me sigh. He looked like a tan Henry Cavill. All I could say was thank God for Kimmy's food diary.

Chapter 5: Xander

"Again! Again!" Coach Renitsky yelled after another failed attempt on our new jump combination. "Kimmy, more height. You are underrotating the double toe loop."

Kimmy nodded but didn't respond. It was kind of unlike her not to have some sort of comedic retort. But then again, it was unlike her to miss so many jumps in a row. She had been extra tired and drinking those awful energy drinks every chance she got for a week now. I was starting to worry about her.

"Hey, you okay?" I asked, skating up to her.

"Yeah, I'm fine. I just wish he'd lay off me," she said with her hands on her knees as she tried to catch her breath.

I placed my hand on her back and said, "Hey, Kim, if you're not feeling well, let's just call it a night and go home."

"No!" she yelled, smacking my hand away. "If you can do it, I can do it."

"It's not a matter of if I can do it or not. On a normal day I know you could, but you're obviously sick. Just take a couple of days off until you feel better."

"Alexander," Renitsky yelled. "Show her! Show her what the combination looks like."

"She knows what it looks like. She doesn't feel well."

"I feel fine!" she yelled stubbornly.

I rolled my eyes. "Whatever," I said as I gathered speed to go into the double Axel, double toe loop combination.

"See!" Renitsky yelled. "Perfect rotation. Try it again. Together."

I grabbed Kimmy's hand to lead her into position. In the routine, the buildup to the jumps started with us holding hands and then separating just seconds before the double Axel. When I touched Kimmy's hand this time, however, it was extremely cold. Sure, we were on the ice and that might not have been strange normally, but Kimmy's hands were never this cold, especially after we had been skating for two hours. I dropped her hand and touched her forehead. Once again freezing. It was like she was a dead body. I knew something wasn't right. "Renitsky, we're done. Kimmy is sick," I yelled into the stands where he sat.

Kimmy tried to protest, but instead her eyes rolled into the back of her head and her body went limp. I lifted her up and carried her off the ice.

Trying not to panic, I set her down on a bench and made sure she was breathing. One of the rink staff members approached with a first aid kit. "What happened?" she asked. "Did she fall?"

"No, she just fainted," I said.

The woman felt her wrist and then her neck. "Call 911. I can't find a pulse!" she yelled before immediately starting chest compressions.

"What do you mean you can't find a pulse?" I asked. There was no more trying not to panic. I was definitely panicking. The room starting spinning and I couldn't breathe. What did she mean there was no pulse? Did that mean Kimmy was dead or something?

"Does she have any allergies?" someone asked.

"No, no. I don't think so."

Suddenly, I looked around and I was in an ambulance. I didn't even remember the paramedics arriving or me getting in with Kimmy's lifeless body. Everything was moving so fast, everything except Kimmy who hadn't moved since passing out in my arms.

"Any drugs?" someone else asked.

"Like, is she on drugs?" I asked to clarify. "No, she doesn't do drugs. She's been drinking energy drinks a lot lately."

"And is that out of the ordinary?"

"Yes, she's been really tired so she started drinking energy drinks. I told her that stuff was poison. Is that what happened?"

The paramedic shook his head. "We don't know what is happening, but I don't think it's about an energy drink."

"But it could be, right?" I said, clutching my head. "What if she had a heart attack? I heard about this high school kid once who drank a bunch of energy drinks and coffee and he had a heart attack. Is my sister having a heart attack? This is my fault."

"Hey, you're gonna have to pull yourself together. She's not having a heart attack," the paramedic said.

"Her blood pressure is dropping again," the other one said. "She needs a transfusion now."

"Are you a match to your sister, son?" the first paramedic asked.

I shrugged. "I don't know."

When we got to the hospital, I felt like I was caught in another whirlwind. Kimmy was whisked off while another person—a nurse or administrator or something like that—started asking me a bunch of questions. While answering these questions, my mother arrived.

"What happened to her?" she asked. "Did she fall and hurt herself?" she added in Russian. It was classic Nadia Vaughn to ask that part in Russian. It was like she didn't want the hospital staff to know that her daughter might have fallen during a skating routine. As if anyone cared. But to my mom, what mattered most was that her children were perfect. We weren't allowed to make mistakes.

"No, Mom, it's worse. It's so much worse," I said. I can't remember if I was speaking English or Russian to her. I just remember concentrating on breathing in and out so I didn't burst into tears of fear for my sister.

An hour later, a doctor approached us in the waiting room.

"Is she okay?" I asked before she even introduced herself.

"I'm Dr. Roche," she said by way of introduction. "Your sister—daughter—gave us quite a scare. We gave her an emergency blood transfusion and she's stable now. She's awake and even talking. Do you want to see her?"

I didn't even vocalize an answer as I started walking down the hall toward where I saw them take her.

"What is wrong with her?" my mother asked.

"We don't know for sure. We're still running tests."

"If you had to guess?" I asked.

Dr. Roche sighed. "Her hemoglobin, red blood cells, white blood cells and platelets are extremely low."

"How low?" I interrupted as if I would understand any information she would proceed to give me. I just needed to feel informed.

She stopped walking and said, "Hemoglobin was 3, her red and white, 1.2 and 1.3 respectively, and her platelets were at 17,000."

I didn't know what any of that meant and it probably showed on my face because Dr. Roche added, "Just for a point of reference, hemoglobin should be between 12 and 14. Red and white blood cells should be between 4.2 and 5.4 and platelets should be between 150,000 to 450,000."

My jaw dropped. I knew nothing about medicine, but I knew those numbers were not good.

"Because of these levels," Dr. Roche said, "we suspect a form of blood cancer or perhaps bone marrow failure."

"Cancer?" my mother said. "Kimbra has cancer? She will have to lose her hair?"

Both the doctor and I stared at my mother. What an odd and inappropriate thing to be worried about at a time like this.

"Um, we have her scheduled for a bone biopsy in the morning so we can make sure."

"In the morning?" I asked. "Why not now?"

"The oncologist tried, but there is hardly any bone marrow to extract from your sister right now. We should have better success in the morning."

"Should?" I asked. "So there's no guarantee? What if she doesn't have enough marrow then either?"

"We'll cross that bridge when we come to it."

"She has to stay the night?" my mother asked.

"Yes, definitely," the doctor said as she continued to lead us to Kimmy's room. Apparently, she had already been moved out of the emergency room.

I entered Kimmy's hospital room to see her looking so much better than she had the past week. During her Red Bull phase she had looked so pale and weak. I should have realized sooner that something was really wrong with her.

But now, she looked great. There was color in her cheeks and she actually looked like she had a bit of energy ... without an energy drink.

"God, Kim," I said upon entering her room with exaggerated exasperation, "Mom and Patrick are never going to buy you a car if you start fainting all over the place."

She smirked. "Whatever. I'll just take your car."

My mom hugged her and said, "The doctor says you are all better."

"That's not what I said at all," Dr. Roche said. "You're stable but we need to do more testing."

"Wait. I can't go home?" Kimmy asked.

"No, we are testing you for—"

"You can go home in the morning," my mother interrupted the doctor. Was she trying to hide what was really happening? I guessed she was just trying to protect Kimmy, but I didn't see how it was helpful. She was sixteen, plenty old enough to understand what was happening to her.

"Ugh, I just want to go home," Kimmy said. "God, I'm still in my tights and leotard."

"I'll go home and get you a change of clothes, okay?" my mother said. She kissed her on the forehead then grabbed the doctor by the elbow and led her out the door.

I sat down on Kimmy's bed and said, "Seriously, you scared the crap out of me, kid."

"And I couldn't get the combination right either."

"Hey, don't worry about that now. Just focus on getting better."

"If I'm going home in the morning, maybe I can get to the rink tomorrow afternoon and try again," she said as if she didn't even hear me. She was not going to let this go. Somehow she was convinced that we needed this combination in order to win Nationals.

When I looked at her sitting in that hospital bed, all I could see was the six-year-old little girl so obsessed with ice skating that she would wear her skates in the house. Fortunately, she had used a blade cover ... most of the time.

~~~

I remembered the day she decided she was going to the Olympics. She had just finished a marathon of watching ice skating routines, mostly Marci Wong performances.

"That's going to be me," she had said.

"Really?" I said. "And how are you going to make sure that happens?" I asked in my eight-year-old wisdom.

"I will practice every day for the rest of my life if I have to. I will skate for eight hours a day."

"Well, we won't be able to see each other very often."

"Why not?" she asked, looking up at me with her light blue eyes.

"Well, you have to go to school for eight hours and then if you skate for another eight hours, you will have to go right to bed after and we won't see each other."

Kimmy thought about this for a few moments. I knew she was trying to think of a solution. For all intents and purposes, I was her favorite person in the house. There wasn't really a question about that. She had to figure out a way for us to be together.

"I got it," she said. "I just won't go to school. I don't need to go to school to be a figure skater."

"Um, you have to go to school. It's the law. If you don't, our parents go to jail."

"Mom too?" she asked for clarification. I nodded. "Fine, then why don't we skate together?" Her eyes lit up, impressed with her own idea. "We could be a brother-sister team like Kitty and Peter Carruthers. That way, we can be together all the time!"

I smirked and shook my head. There was no way I was going to be a figure skater. Sure, I could skate. I was pretty good at it too. Not only could I out skate everyone on my hockey team, but I, on my own, was able to differentiate each of the six types of figure skating jumps and I had successfully attempted them all. And that was without training. I wondered what I would be able to do with a little help from a coach. So out of pure curiosity, I joined Kimmy on her first ice skating lesson a week later.

I fell in love with the sport in that very first lesson. At first, we did in fact skate for nearly eight hours a day. It was summer and so that was okay. At the end of that summer, our skating club had an exhibition. Kimmy and I performed a routine to "Pocket Full of Sunshine" by Natasha Bedingfield. It wasn't anything special. I mean, we had only been skating together for two months. But apparently, it was so impressive that we got a standing ovation. People even threw flowers and teddy bears on the ice as if we had just skated a gold-medal winning performance. That was it for Kimmy. She was sold. Ice skating had been her life from that moment on. And though I had never wanted to admit it, it had become my life too.

~~~

I pulled the recliner chair that was in her hospital room next to her bed and tried to get comfortable. My mother had already come back with a change of clothes for Kimmy and had left again. I had no plans of leaving though. If Kimmy was here, I was here. There was no way I was going to leave her alone. We flipped through the channels for nearly an hour, arguing about what to watch when suddenly, she grew quiet. I looked over at her and noticed that her skin was really red and she was taking rather short, shallow breaths.

"Kim, what's wrong?"

With tears in her eyes she shook her head. "I can't ... breathe ... "

"Somebody help! Somebody help me!" I yelled into the hallway after manically pressing the call button. A nurse rushed past me into the room.

"What happened?" she asked

"I don't know. She says she can't breathe."

Two more people rushed into the room and surrounded Kimmy's bed, pushing me out of the way in the process.

"There's fluid in her lungs."

"Page Dr. Roche."

"Xander?" Nurse James said. "Xander, we need you to step outside."

"What's going on? What happened? She was fine a second ago."

"And she'll be fine again soon. She's having a reaction to the blood transfusion we gave her earlier," he said.

"What? Why?"

"We don't know. But we need you to step outside right now. As soon as I know anything else, I'll make sure we let you know, okay?" I nodded and stepped outside. I stayed as close as possible though so I could hear what was happening in the room.

Chapter 6: Bria

I paced back and forth in the stands for a few seconds. Then I sat down and put my green headphones on. I was listening to Debussy to calm me down. After a few seconds I took off he headphones and started pacing again. Where were they? They never missed their rink time. They paid for it monthly so missing two hours of rink time would not be fiscally responsible, right?

Maybe they overslept. I should call them. I took out my phone and remembered the last time I had seen his phone number on it. It was when he broke up with me via text. I couldn't call him. He wouldn't want me to.

Maybe I could call Kimmy, I thought. Hmph. And say what? "Hey, I've been following your brother for like nine months and I'm wondering why he's not at the rink right now so I can leer at him with his shirt off."

I put my phone away and sat down again. Calling made absolutely no sense and could possibly get me arrested for stalking.

There had to be a reason why they weren't there. I needed to come up with a theory and then do an experiment to see if it was true. What if it was something as simple as they decided to change rinks? Cherry Hill Rink wasn't the only ice skating rink in the area. I had a theory; now time to test it.

I saw the security guard drinking a cup of coffee near the entrance, so I went over to him and said, "Um, I'm a reporter for the Cherry Hill High newspaper and I'm doing a story on Kimmy and Xander Vaughn."

"Yeah, I've seen you here before," he said in a thick Russian accent. I imagined he probably spoke Russian to Xander all the time. Why? I didn't know. Just had a feeling.

"So, um, where are they today?"

"Well, little Kimbra took ill last night and they took her to hospital," he said.

"Is she okay?"

He shrugged. "I have not heard one way or the other. But if it was really bad I'm sure Xander would have told me." Ah, I knew it. They did talk. "Look, why don't you just call him and ask if she okay?" he said.

"It's not that big of a deal. I mean, I'm sure she's fine. I can write the article another day. No biggie. It's not that important. It's not like I don't have other things I can write about." Real smooth, Bria. You sound like a psycho.

I sounded like a psycho and I felt like a jerk. All morning I had only been concerned about Xander and barely even thought about Kimmy.

Kimmy was sick and went to the hospital yesterday. Was she still there? Was she home now? Where was Xander? It had to be slightly serious because if it wasn't, Xander would have come to skate without her. Should I go to the hospital? Now that would be creepy. The better plan would be to go to school and hope that he was there. If he was there, I would even gather the courage to ask him about his sister.

But at school, his car wasn't in the parking lot. Well, his parents could have dropped him off. Maybe he was there after all. I changed my route to class in order to purposely run into him going to his classes but to no avail.

He wasn't there, which meant something serious was happening.

Chapter 7: Xander

The same blood transfusion that returned Kimmy's energy and made her feel normal again also caused an extremely dangerous reaction which led to the scary emergency from the night before. After several hours on oxygen, she was stabilized. They started her on a bunch of drugs to try to stimulate blood production, but apparently that was just a temporary solution.

"I'm scared, Xan," Kimmy said with glistening eyes the next day. They had just finished a biopsy that was so painful she cried for twenty minutes.

"I know. I am too, princess," I said, sitting on the bed and putting my arm around her.

Looking up at me she said, "You haven't called me 'princess' since last summer."

I nodded. "When you got a boyfriend, I assumed you had grown out of it."

Kimmy shook her head. "I'll never grow out of it." She buried her head in my chest and cried.

"Shh. It's okay, princess. I'm gonna take care of you. I'll always take care of you."

"What's happening, Xan? Why won't they tell me what's wrong with me?"

"I don't know."

"They're treating me like a child. They won't tell me anything."

"I wish I could tell you what I know but I don't even understand what they've told me. All I know is that your blood isn't doing what it's supposed to do so they gave you a blood transfusion but then you had a bad reaction to it and something went wrong with your lungs."

"Sweet Cheez-Its, Xan. Am I gonna die?"

My heart was breaking. I had no idea what to tell her. I didn't know how to explain what was going on; I didn't even understand it myself. But I knew who would. Bria Browning. She was so smart she probably knew exactly what was happening and if she didn't, she would just research it until she did.

Pride, fear, and embarrassment had kept me from calling Bria for nearly a year. But my feelings didn't matter anymore. Not when my little sister was suffering. If Bria could offer Kimmy even a little assurance that she would be okay, it would be worth the trauma of facing the girl who broke my heart.

I didn't know whether to call her or go to her house to see her in person. What was the protocol for asking your ex-girlfriend, who made it perfectly clear that she never wanted to see you again and who you hadn't spoken to for nearly a year, for a favor?

As I stood in the hallway outside of Kimmy's hospital room, with Bria's number typed into my phone, something amazing happened. Bria Browning walked right up to me.

We stared at each other until one of us said, "Hey." Or it could have been both of us. I can't be sure.

Another moment passed before I said, "What are you doing here?"

"I heard about Kimmy," she said. "Everyone at school is talking about it, since you didn't come in today. I came to see how she's doing. If that's okay. I can go if it's not. Should I go?"

"No, no, no. I was actually just about to call you," I said, holding up my phone as evidence.

"Why?" she asked.

Because I love you and I miss you, and I need you in my life, and I need to hear your voice and your weird, yet genius theories. And when you're close to me my skin tingles and I feel like I can fly. I wanted to say all of that, but instead I said, "Kimmy is really scared and no one will give her a straight answer about what's really happening. I thought you could answer some questions for her."

"I'm not a doctor," she said in her matter-of-fact tone.

"I know, but you're the smartest person we know and I know you'll tell us the truth about what you do know and research anything you don't."

Bria looked around then asked, "Where are your parents?"

"They are talking to an oncologist."

Her eyes widened.

"That's bad, isn't?" I asked.

"Yes," she said. Her honesty was scary but refreshing. "What else have you heard?"

I took a deep breath and tried to recall all the words that had been swirling around last night and this morning: hemoglobin, red blood cells, plastic, 45nemia, transplant, pulmonary edamame, and bone marrow.

Bria nodded every few seconds at my word salad of medical terms as if she were making mental calculations. Her beautiful mind was at work.

"First of all, I think you mean aplastic anemia and pulmonary edema,"

"Yeah, that sounds right."

"Second, give me a minute to look up a couple of things." She took out her phone and started typing. Bria spent about five minutes typing into her phone while I just stared at her. It was Thursday which meant a green pair of

Beats headphones and a green backpack which she paired with a green plaid skirt, a black turtleneck and knee high black boots. I know I focused on her clothes a lot; I just always thought she was so unique and well put together. I had no idea why she got picked on at school. She wasn't poor, as evidenced by the different pair of $300 headphones she wore every day. She was far from ugly. She was kind and considerate to everyone, and she was without question the smartest person in school. The only explanation was that the other kids were either jealous or racist.

"Okay. Can I see her now?" she asked a few minutes later, pulling me out of my compulsive staring.

"Oh, yeah, yeah, yeah." I stepped aside and followed her into Kimmy's room.

Bria hugged Kimmy then sat next to her on the bed. They were good friends when Bria and I were dating, almost like sisters. It took two weeks before I even told Kimmy that I was dating Bria, but once I did, she had been totally on board with keeping it a secret from my parents and constantly covered for me.

"How are you feeling?" Bria asked.

"Tired. Scared," Kimmy responded.

"You are probably tired because your blood count is way too low. And you are understandably scared because your doctors are not telling you what's going on. They can't do that to you no matter what your parents tell them. You are sixteen and more than old enough to have a say in your treatment options and decisions about your body."

I knew Bria wasn't a doctor, but the way she was able to speak to Kimmy and reassure her was more effective than any actual doctor that I had ever met.

"I'm going to explain the terms your brother has been hearing and give you the right questions to ask your doctors and your parents. That's all I can do."

Kimmy nodded, "That's all I want."

During the next thirty minutes, Kimmy stared straight ahead while Bria explained what was possibly happening to her.

"So I have aplastic anemia?" Kimmy asked.

"That's what it sounds like."

"And I'll need a bone marrow transplant?"

Bria nodded.

"They tested me this morning," I said. "I can donate, right?"

"That will be the best solution. A sibling match is ideal," Bria said.

"What if he doesn't match?" Kimmy asked.

"I'll match," I said.

~~~

After Bria left, I asked, "Are you okay?"

Kimmy nodded. "I'm better than okay."

"Really?"

"Yes. It's like ... It's like I understand the enemy. So I'm great."

"What do you mean?"

"Remember when we competed in the Denver Invitational and there was this new pairs couple in the competition and they were really freaking me out because I kept hearing how amazing they were and how they were really going to destroy us, but I had never seen them skate before? And then I went on YouTube and saw videos of their performances, and I saw with my own eyes how ridiculously incredible they were."

"I don't get it."

"I stopped freaking out even though the rumors were true. I stopped freaking out because I finally knew what I was up against. I understood the competition. And did we or did we not kick their asses in the finals?"

I smiled. "We did."

"Just like we're gonna kick aplastic anemia's ass," she said with the Kimmy drive and determination I was used to.

"And we're gonna do it together."

Chapter 8: Xander

Apparently, Kimmy's condition was so serious that they put a rush on my blood work and we found out the next day that I wasn't a match.

"It's okay, princess. We'll find a match," I said. "You're not gonna die."

"You never know," she said weakly. She was still having trouble breathing. "I could beat this and then get hit by a car as I'm walking out of the hospital."

I felt like I had been hit in the gut. I had never heard her be so negative. What was happening to my happy-go-lucky baby sister? Even the spirit she had displayed yesterday after talking to Bria had somehow died.

"I need a favor," she said suddenly.

"Anything."

"Remember that time we were in that secondhand shop in Portland right after Junior Regionals?" she asked.

"Yeah, I remember."

"I found this hand stitched silver and purple sequined jacket there. It was amazing. One of a kind. But I didn't get it, because I thought it was too much. Not that it cost too much but that the jacket itself was just too much of an eye grabber, you know? Like people would say, 'Who does she think she is?' if I were to, like, wear this jacket down the street. So I didn't get it. And then we went back to the hotel that night and I couldn't stop thinking about it. I literally had a dream about it. The next day, I made Mom take me back to the shop so I could get it and it was gone. I still think about that jacket all the time. I should have just bought it when I first saw it. Now it's gone forever."

"Do you want me to go find this jacket? Maybe I can look on eBay or something."

"This is not about a stupid jacket!" she yelled.

"Well it kind of seems like it is since you've been talking about it for like five minutes straight," I said.

"My point, Xander, is that it has been two years and I still regret a jacket that I missed out on. A stupid jacket. So I can't imagine what you must feel about Bria."

"Bria?"

"Yes, Bria. When she was in here yesterday you almost exploded with joy."

"I ...What do you ... " Was it that obvious? I thought I hid it better. After a year of not seeing her up close and suddenly being in the same room with her and her adorably cute self what was I supposed to do? I was just proud of myself for not wrapping her in a bear hug and sniffing her hair.

"This is my favor," Kimmy said. "Please go tell Bria how you feel."

I sighed. "I don't know if I can."

"Why not?"

I sat down at the foot of her bed. "That night just replays in my head. The things Patrick said about her. There is nothing I can say that can excuse or even explain that kind of hate. And then instead of trying, I just avoided her. I just accepted the end of our relationship. I didn't fight for her. She has to think I'm some sort of coward."

"You never know until you talk to her. Besides, I didn't give you an option. You said you'd do me a favor and this is the favor so hop to it," she said.

"Now?"

"Yes, now. Go!"

"Okay, I'm going."

Several seconds later, Kimmy said, "You haven't moved."

"I haven't?"

Kimmy took a pillow and threw it at my head. "Get out!"

"I'm out. I'm out," I said, ducking out of her room. I stood in the hallway, thinking about Bria. What on earth could I say that would explain why I had avoided her for almost a year? There was nothing that could explain that. There was no excuse. The only thing I could do was what Kim asked me to. Tell her how I felt.

~~~

Honestly, I had rehearsed a speech to Bria in my head thousands of times. But now that I was actually planning on saying it, the words didn't make sense in my head. Sentences were popping up out of order. I had no idea what was happening to my brain as I drove to school.

I knew she would be there even though classes had ended an hour ago. She stayed there as long as possible even when she didn't have a chess match or yearbook or newspaper. She hated being at home, complaining that it was too quiet for her to think. She would rather sit outside the band room during their rehearsal and read a book than sit at home alone in her room.

I parked next to her car and waited for her, but then I decided that was too creepy. Sitting in my big, black SUV it looked like I was about to kidnap her. I got out and stood next to her car, but that just looked sad. I was about to leave when I heard a voice say, "Is Kimmy all right?" It was Bria.

"No, yes, she's fine. For now."

And then we just stared at each other. It was Friday which meant white Beats headphones and a white backpack which she paired with a black skirt and a black hoodie.

"You're not a sequined jacket," I blurted after a few seconds. Most people would be visibly confused by such a random statement, but not my Bria. I could practically see her brain working, trying to make the connection as to why I would compare her to a sequined jacket.

"What I meant to say is that I ... I love you," I said when my brain finally started working again.

"You love me more than sequins?"

"Yes, no, I mean ... Forget the sequins. I'm trying to tell you that I'm in love with you, Ambria Browning."

She paused. "How do you know?"

Not the response I was hoping for but it was a very Bria thing to say. She analyzed and evaluated everything. It was part of what I loved about her.

"I know because I haven't felt whole since the last time I touched you. I know I love you because no matter what I do or how hard I try, I can't stop thinking about you. Every day, day in and day out, I think about you and what you're doing and if you're thinking about me too."

"Why?" she asked simply. Once again, it didn't offend me. It didn't even make me nervous. In fact, her questions made me feel better. These were feelings I had been holding in for over a year. Saying it out loud was cathartic.

"Bria, I love the way your mind works. I love the way you think. I love how you make everything clear. I love seeing the world through your eyes. I love that you're so real and honest. You've never lied to me or tried to manipulate me. I love that when I'm with you I can be me."

"Maybe that just means we are or should be really good friends."

"Then why do I want to kiss you so badly?"

She paused then asked, "What if I don't feel the same way?"

"I think you do," I said.

"How do you know?"

"Bria, you wake up every day at 5 a.m. to drive halfway across town to watch me skate."

Her eyes expanded in shock.

"Yes, I know. Do you really think I wouldn't notice a random black girl sitting in the stands of an ice skating rink every morning? I had to tell the security guard you were with me so he wouldn't kick you out."

Bria rolled her lips in until they made a straight line just like she did when she was in trouble during a chess match. She wouldn't be able to outthink my logic. "And don't even try to say you come to watch Kimbra or to see both of us 'cause you always leave after my solo workout."

Bria sighed. "Okay, fine. I come to see you."

"Why?" I asked. Now it was my turn for questions. I needed to hear how she felt. I needed to know if she still loved me.

"Because you make me feel," she said, her voice shaking.

"Feel what?"

"Everything! You make me feel everything." Bria dropped the newspapers she had been carrying and covered her face with her hands as tears streamed down her cheeks.

Instinctively, I wrapped her in my arms. "My life is so empty," she said into my chest through her tears. "I'm alone all the time. My parents barely know I'm alive. It's like we're casual roommates who don't even like each other instead of a family. But when I'm with you," she said, looking up at me, "I feel needed and wanted. I feel special. And even when you dumped me, I felt angry, and scared, and jealous of every single being that got to be near you that wasn't me. And those feelings, painful as they may be, were better than the nothing I felt when you weren't around."

"Wait a minute, Bria. What are you talking about? I didn't dump you. You dumped me."

Bria pulled away and wiped wetness from her eyes. "Xander, you texted me that night and told me you couldn't see me anymore. I think I would remember that. It nearly destroyed me. I cried for a week."

"A text?"

"Yes, a text. I know it's cruel, but I just figured your parents made you do it or threatened to take away skating or something. I didn't blame you."

Tears burned behind my eyes. My heart felt like a stone in my chest. "Bria, there is nothing my parents could say to make me break up with you. I would have given up skating in a heartbeat. That's how much you meant..." I swallowed hard to keep my voice from cracking. "That's how much you mean to me. I, honestly, don't know what hurts more, the fact that I have been without you for a year because of a fake text or the idea that you think I could break up with you in a text. I swear I would never hurt you like that," I said, looking into her eyes. "*You* broke up with *me* in a letter."

"A letter?"

"Yeah, it was a letter on your favorite stationery. You said you thought my dad was a racist and you couldn't subject yourself to such an environment and that if I really cared about you, I would stay away from you until you were ready to talk to me again," I said, reciting the exact words of the letter I had read a hundred times before burning in a fire.

Bria shook her head slowly. "You think I broke up with you in a letter? Was it handwritten or typed?"

I thought about it for a moment. "It was typed." I had never thought about it before. I was in too much pain to think logically at that point. Even though it was on her personal stationery, since it was typed, it technically could have come from anyone.

"Xander, I never wrote a letter like that. That's not even what I believe about racism."

I felt sick to my stomach. I couldn't believe what I was hearing. She didn't break up with me? I thought I was respecting her wishes by staying away from her. It was the least I could do considering the way my father had treated her. But it wasn't her wish. She hadn't rejected me and I had just lived the past year of my life without her for no reason? On top of that, she had spent that entire time thinking a was some kind of heartless jerk that breaks up with girls in a text message.

"Do you still love me, Bria?" I asked still fighting back my tears.

"Yeah. I do," she said, nodding.

I couldn't wait any longer. I had to kiss her.

Chapter 9: Bria

Not ready to let each other go but also not wanting to freeze to death, we decided to move our reunion to Xander's car. I sat in the back seat and he rested his head in my lap and stared up at me. God, I had missed seeing those eyes close-up. There was nothing else like them in the world. A turquoise blue so deep they could paralyze me with just a glance.

"How are your parents?" he asked as we tried to catch up on the past year of our lives.

I shrugged. "The same."

"That sucks," he said. "Do you have a new theory?" I smiled. He remembered how I liked to create theories in advance of analyzing my problems. I lived my life by the scientific method.

"Actually, I do. I call it the Treadmill Theory."

Xander smiled. "I've missed your theories."

I leaned over and kissed him before beginning my explanation. "In January, every year people make New Year's resolutions to lose weight. They buy these treadmills with this vision of their future selves in their minds. But then they see how much work a treadmill is, and they become disillusioned with it. It starts to get ignored and soon it becomes just a home accessory that holds pantyhose and bathrobes."

"Are you comparing yourself to a treadmill?" he asked.

"Well you compared me to a sequined jacket," I said, smiling.

"That's fair. Continue."

"My theory is that my parents never really wanted kids. They liked the idea of this perfect family unit. But then when they realized how much work it would be they checked out as soon as they could. And now I'm just an accessory that they bring out for photo ops when necessary."

"I'm sorry, Bree," he said, intertwining our fingers and kissing the inside of my wrist. "You are never gonna be alone again."

I wasn't as sure as he was about that. This was our senior year of high school. I was going off to college. He was probably going off to skate around the world. There was no way he could guarantee we would be together. I chose not to bring that up though. There would be time to worry about the future later. Right now was the time to enjoy having my Xander back. I felt so euphoric my whole body tingled. "What about your parents?"

"Worse," he said.

"How is that even possible?"

"They started using Kimmy to spy on me."

"I'm sorry, Xan." I sighed. "How is Kimmy? Did they diagnose her?"

Instantly, tears welled in his eyes. He cleared his throat, composed himself a little and said, "It's definitely aplastic anemia. She needs someone to donate bone marrow and I'm not a match."

"This is not your fault, Xander. Do not blame yourself for the cards genetics dealt you," I said, kissing his forehead.

"I'm her big brother. I'm supposed to protect her. This was the one thing I could have done to save her life. Why didn't I match?" He squeezed my hand as if he needed to hang on to me to keep from falling off the edge of the world.

"Not all siblings are a genetic match. In fact, there is only a 25 percent chance that a sibling will be a genetic bone marrow match."

"But if I'm her brother, and we have the same parents and I only have a 25 percent chance of matching her, isn't there less of a chance for some random person to match?"

"Not really. There are many factors like genetics and race that go into it and make the odds much higher. If she were Asian or mixed race or something, it would be a lot harder. But because Kimmy is white she actually has about a 77 percent chance of finding a donor match with the registry."

"Really?"

"Yeah, I read about it today. I can do more research on it if you want."

"I missed you so much, Bria Bear," he said smiling up at me.

"I missed you too, Xanadu."

"I love you," he said as if he just needed to make that clear again. "And I will tell you that ten times a day to make up for the year together we've missed out on."

"Ten months, three weeks and four days," I corrected him.

"Whatever. Just tell me you love me," he said.

"I love you," I said.

He smiled. "Say it again."

"I love you."

"Again."

"I love you, I love you, I love you," I said, kissing him again and again.

Matchless

Chapter 10: Xander

Bria was such a surprise in my life when I met her a year and a half ago. We had just started our junior year at Cherry Hill High but we weren't friends. I don't think we had ever even spoken. I, of course, knew who she was. In fact, her dad was my pediatrician until I was like five or something. We probably played together when we were little. By the time high school rolled around, our roads had completely diverged. I knew her as the girl who had gotten a perfect score on the SATs, a feat that had gotten her a segment on the local news. Now it was my turn to be featured on that same local news segment after Kimmy and I had placed third in the World Junior Championships. It was our first big win since Kimmy had met the age requirement to compete and Cherry Hill High wanted to capitalize on the publicity. So they sent a reporter from the school newspaper to my rink to interview me. That reporter was Bria Browning.

She was different than any other girl I had met up until that point. She had this air about her that I couldn't quite define. It wasn't arrogance or haughtiness, but maybe just a personal assurance or confidence in herself that made her believe that even if she didn't have the answer to something, she could figure it out. Whatever the quality was, this thing she had that I couldn't name, it was sexy as hell.

"You're really good, but you're skating for your sister and not yourself," she said after watching me practice.

"What are you talking about?"

"Look, it's just a theory, but I've watched tape of you skating and I've seen your interviews. I could probably write this entire story about you without even talking to you."

"I see you've done your research on me," I said flirtatiously. It hadn't escaped me that she was also super cute. How could someone be so sexy and so cute at the same time? It was mind boggling. Her hair was in two super curly pigtails that I just wanted to squeeze. She wore white socks that went up to her knees and met with a checkered skirt paired with a hooded red sweater that looked like it was straight out of the movie E.T. She gave off this whole 80s' comic book girl vibe that seemed completely unintentional, which made it even more adorable somehow.

Plus, I had just broken up with Melanie Cummings, a figure skater from Los Angeles who I had met at an invitational in Portland, Oregon. Long-distance relationships didn't really work out at age sixteen. Everyone at school thought I had just made her up. Not that I dated her just to tell my friends. Okay, well, a part of me did. A part of me needed people to know that I could get a girlfriend. I was a scrawny skating freak with a big head who never had time to go to parties and didn't have many friends at all.

"It's what I do. I research." She totally didn't pick up on my flirting. "Anyway," she continued, "you're an amazing skater. You're competing and winning internationally, but hardly anyone at school even knows what you do. When you do interviews, you let your sister do all the talking as if she's the star when, according to the experts, you are technically much more advanced than she is. You could easily win in a solo career. My theory is, either you don't love skating and you only do it for your sister or you are ashamed of it for some reason."

I stared at her in shock. It was like she was reading my mind. How the hell was she able to figure that out just by observing video tapes of my interviews and some recordings of my performances?

"Well, if I'm being honest with myself, I do hold back a little."

"Why?" she asked.

"I don't know."

"Yes, you do," she said. I couldn't get over how pointedly she said it. She was so confident and so absolutely correct that it was a little intimidating.

"Okay, fine. I'm a little afraid that ... this is embarrassing." I paused a moment to try to read her reaction. I wanted there to be a sign as to whether I should reveal the truth to her or not. I barely knew her; why was I about to tell her something so absolutely personal? But if I was looking for a reaction in Bria, I was out of luck. She was completely stone-faced. I felt like I could tell her anything and she wouldn't judge me one way or the other. "I think I'm afraid that if I show how much I really love skating that people will think I'm gay. There have already been rumors at school. So, I don't tell people I skate. And when they find out, I hide behind my sister. I make it seem like I only do it for her."

Bria pursed her lips together and nodded. "There are only two possible outcomes from that line of reasoning," she said. "Either one, you *are* gay, and the rumors are correct. In which case, who cares? Congrats to the alien high schoolers who actually figured out something correctly. Or two, you are *not* gay and the rumors are incorrect, in which case, who cares? The aliens got it wrong just like most of the decisions in their lives."

"Alien high schoolers?" I asked.

She nodded. "I have a theory that high school is another planet and high school students are aliens. That is the only explanation for the weird stuff that happens there." She shrugged. "So far nothing has proved me wrong. Therefore, why would I care what the aliens believe?"

I chuckled a little and then more. She had to be joking, right? Everyone cared about what their peers thought or did I just meet the first girl who honestly didn't?

Bria didn't crack a smile. She was dead serious. And after I thought about it for a moment, I realized she was right. Who the hell cared? I stopped laughing and stared at her. I felt lighter. I felt free. Who cared what people ... or aliens thought? Why was that such a novel idea for me?

"There's one more reason why I hold back," I said, suddenly feeling like I was in a therapy session and I needed to pour out my soul to this girl. "I think I'm afraid that if I put myself out there by myself and I fail, I'll have no one to blame but myself. Not that I would ever blame Kim for us not winning. It's just it's less scary when you're not alone."

Bria nodded. "I get that. Spoiled milk."

"What?" I asked. Maybe I had judged this girl wrong. She could be insane. Why was she talking about spoiled milk?

"I have a spoiled milk theory. Have you ever gone to pour milk on your cereal and there is only a little left, not enough for a whole bowl? You pour some on your cereal but leave a little in the carton so that you're not the one to finish it off, right? But then everyone after you sees how little is left and they don't use it either until finally the milk is spoiled and no one gets to use it. It's almost as if you'd prefer to have a tiny bit of spoiled milk in reserve instead of getting the full use of the good milk when you can."

"Why save myself? I could go bad," I said as I translated her analogy for my situation. "I could get injured and never be able to skate again. Then what use was what I saved? Spoiled milk."

Bria snapped her fingers and pointed at me, indicating that I had gotten the point.

Holy hell. I understood her ridiculous theory. Wow. In the span of about five minutes, Bria had correctly evaluated my entire skating career. We ended up talking for three more hours about everything and I mean everything. I was addicted to conversation with her. She had a way of taking something that seemed complicated, something that totally stressed me out, and explaining it simply. I couldn't get enough of her and I didn't want the night to end.

"Do you skate?" I asked her.

Smiling shyly she said, "Actually, the last time I skated I think it was with you."

"What? What are you talking about? I think I would remember that."

"Well, think hard," she said while scrolling through her phone. "Think back about twelve years." Bria held out her phone for me. I took it and stared at a picture of us at four years old holding hands and ice skating.

"Oh my God. Where did you find this?"

"Part of my research, man. I got skills."

Her attempt at colloquial speech sounded so fake that we both laughed. "Seriously though, when I found out I was interviewing you, I remembered that I had been at your four-year-old birthday party. After some digging, I found this picture. Cute, right?"

"Adorable. We looked good together. Why have we not been close since?"

Bria shrugged. "No idea."

I stared at the picture for a long time. Something didn't feel right. We were obviously very close as children. What had happened between our families that would cause us not to talk for twelve years? I wasn't sure what was going on, but somehow I felt that Bria wouldn't be welcome in the Vaughn house. So three weeks later when we officially became a couple, I never told my parents.

Chapter 11: Bria

Xander had enough on his plate. His sister had aplastic anemia and he wasn't a match for the transplant that would save her life. He'd have to drop out of Nationals and put his entire career on hold for who knew how long. There was no plan B when it came to Kimmy and Xander. It was the Olympics or nothing. Which meant he probably hadn't even applied to colleges. Given all that was going on in his world, it was perfectly understandable that he wasn't thinking about who it was that sent the text and the letter that had ended our relationship eleven months ago. But then there's me. I had nothing to do but think ... all the time. And so that was what I did. Actually, I probably did more than just think about the saboteur; I was completely fixated on who or why someone would do something like that.

Who had the motive to break us up? What was that motive? Who had access to Xander's phone to send the text? Who knew where my special stationery was to write that letter? Given those questions, it wasn't hard to come up with a rather short list of suspects.

Kimmy, of course, had the easiest access to both Xander's phone and my stationery, but she had no motive. Unless she thought I was too much of a distraction for her brother. But I never got in the way of their rehearsals and she always seemed so nice to me. I couldn't imagine it was her.

My parents had access to my stationery but not Xander's phone. It couldn't have been them, though. They would actually have to care who I was dating in order to want to break us up. I wasn't even sure if they knew Xander and I were together in the first place. That left Xander's parents, the Vaughns. It made sense. It was Xander's dad after all who went on that racist rant after he caught us making out in his basement. I knew he hated me and everything I stood for. He said as much that night. Xander's mom, Nadia, was a different story. She was never outrightly rude to me, but she was always a bit weird around me. Maybe she was one of those nervous racists. The ones who didn't think they were racist but thought that they were just being realistic and protecting their family from things that went bump in the night.

~~~

I remembered one time in particular about a week before we broke up when I came over to the Vaughn house. Only Xander's car was in their driveway so I felt okay knocking. I couldn't explain why I didn't like to be around his parents at that point. I just didn't like it. Anyway, I knocked on the door but there was no answer. I took out my phone to call him and still no answer. I probably shouldn't have but I tried the door and it was open so I let myself in. There was music coming from the direction of their home gym so I followed it.

When I entered the gym, I immediately regretted it. And not because I was subjected to a blaringly loud and more horrible than usual Rihanna song, but because Xander was shirtless, sweaty, and doing pull-ups to the beat of that Rihanna song.

It was the first time since he'd started working out that I'd seen him without a shirt on. Well, actually, it was the first time I had seen any boy without a shirt on in real life. I had seen guys on TV, but something about seeing someone this close just made me weak. I seriously lost feeling in my face.

I don't know how long I stared at him, but eventually I heard him say, "Hey, Bria. I didn't hear you come in." He dropped to the ground then went to turn off the music that was being projected from his phone through Bluetooth. "I, uh, missed my workout this morning so I was trying to fit it in before you got here. Must have lost track of time," he said by way of explanation as he grabbed a towel and started wiping himself off. I could do nothing but stare at him with my mouth open as he walked toward me. I hoped I wasn't drooling. "I'd hug you, but I reek right now," he said.

"I don't ... It doesn't ... That's okay," I said, stuttering like an idiot.

Xander grinned and tilted his head to the left a little. He walked toward me and said, "In that case, come here." He tugged on my shirt and pulled me to his body then kissed me. He was right: he did reek, but I didn't care. I wrapped my arms around his neck and deepened our kiss. Xander lifted me up and then lowered me to the matted floor.

I whipped my coat off as Xander starting kissing my neck and unbuttoning my shirt. My hands explored the muscular chest that had started this whole thing. I didn't know how far we would go. I didn't want to go all the way. I had a plan for that, but in that moment, I felt that plan going out the window.

We were both half naked and he was on top of me, kissing me at the precise moment when his mom walked in and screamed something in what I assumed to be Russian.

"Mom!" Xander yelled, hopping to his feet.

They continued yelling back and forth for several moments. It was extremely awkward, not only because I didn't know what they were saying but because they were each so angry I thought they might hit each other. Sure, in the interest of learning about my boyfriend's culture, I had learned a few phrases in Russian, but what they were saying was way beyond the basic introductory phrases. But since anger was a universal language, I was able to gather that seeing her half naked son making out with a half naked girl did not please her.

"I am so sorry, Mrs. Vaughn," I said. "I'm not ... This is not ... " I tried to interject. She stopped yelling at Xander and stared at me silently as if she suddenly didn't understand English. "Maybe I should go," I said finally.

"No!" Xander yelled so forcefully that I jumped. "I'm sorry," he said. I could tell he was forcing himself to calm down. "I didn't mean to scare you. I don't want you to go. Stay. Please. I'm gonna take a quick shower. Wait for me, okay?" He turned to his mother and said, "And my mother is going to go to her book club right now. Isn't that right?"

She turned and walked away while muttering in Russian.

"I'm sorry about that, Bria Bear," he said once she was gone. "I'm gonna shower and then maybe we can—"

"Watch a movie?" I volunteered interrupting him.

Xander sighed in frustration. "Bria, come on," he whined.

"I think Spiderman is on Netflix."

He took a deep breath. "Yeah, sure fine. We can watch Spiderman after I take a very, very cold shower." He kissed my forehead then ran upstairs.

As I waited for him to finish his shower, I tried not to imagine him in said shower. Naked. Because most people took showers naked, I would assume that he, too, was naked at that very moment. Just wet and naked. Very naked. To distract myself, I looked around the Vaughns' home gym and even picked up a few of the free weights. It was rather big for a home gym and it smelled really gross. I guessed Mr. Vaughn used it to keep in shape during hockey season. And now Xander was using it to bulk up for skating. And from what I had seen, he had completely succeeded.

"Do your parents know where you are?" I heard a voice say. It was Mrs. Vaughn. I thought she had left.

"Um, no," I said. "But I'm pretty sure they don't care."

"I am pretty sure they will. I am quite positive neither of your parents will approve of this."

I shrugged, wondering what her point was. Was I supposed to care? She obviously didn't understand the dynamic of the Browning household.

Nadia crossed her arms and stared at me. I had no idea what was going on. I could tell she wanted to say something else to me but I didn't know what. I definitely got the idea that she didn't like me. She opened her mouth to say something but then stopped when she heard the bathroom door open upstairs. And that was the first and only conversation I had ever had with Nadia Vaughn ... if you could even call it a conversation.

~~~

In any case, now that I knew the truth, that Xander loved me and didn't intentionally break my heart after all, there was nothing in the world that would make me let him go again. I didn't care what his parents said or did; Xander and I would be together forever.

The next morning, I knew Xander would not be at the rink at 5 a.m. He would most likely be at the hospital. But knowing this didn't stop me from waking up at that ungodly hour anyway. I lay in bed thinking about him and us. All the time we missed all because of my stationery and a stupid text message.

Text message.

I reached for my phone to check. Sure enough, there it was.

Good morning, Beautiful.

It made me so happy I actually started crying. I had missed him even more than I thought possible.

After blubbering like an idiot while staring at my phone for like ten minutes, I swung my legs over the bed and sat up. Holding my phone to my heart, I thought about my stationery. The stationery used to write that bogus letter to Xander. Of course, he would think it was from me, since I was completely addicted to it and used it every chance I got. I used to write him sweet notes and hide them in his backpack.

I don't know why I loved that stationery so much. Who was I kidding? I loved it because it was one of the few gifts my mother had ever given to me. If I thought about it too hard though, it wasn't really a gift so much as a hand-me-down. She had had the stationery made for herself while she was on a shopping trip in France. It had faint black cherry blossom trees with shimmering leaves in the background. And in the bottom right corner in the foreground, our last name Browning was written in elegant script. But when she got home, she decided she didn't like it because they had made the B in Browning too big. It was perfect for me, however, as I would just add an RIA write next to the top part of the B and voilà, it said Bria Browning.

She gave me that stationery when I was thirteen. I still had some left five years later because I only used it for very special occasions. Breaking up with my boyfriend would not have been one of them.

Was it her? Did my mother actually come in my room, take my stationery, and write a fake letter to my boyfriend? Why on Earth would she do that?

Chapter 12: Bria

I hated being called to the office in the middle of class. It wasn't the principal's office but still it was embarrassing and it came with the implication that I had done something wrong. I hadn't. I never did. I was always perfect. And that was probably why no one ever noticed me. No one but Xander. He saw exactly who I was and he not only accepted me the way I was, he loved me.

"Bria! Bria! Bria!" Mrs. Schnauzer the guidance counselor exclaimed in her always over-excited way. Most of the kids in school called her the puppy because she always acted like a puppy happy to see its owner after a long day at work, complete with the bouncing up and down. Or maybe it was because her name was Schnauzer. "It's been so long," she said, gesturing for me to sit down. "Well?" she asked expectantly.

"Well what?"

"Bria, you're too smart to play dumb. College acceptance," she said, clapping her hands together rapidly like she was applauding. "Have you heard back from any of them?"

I nodded, but I didn't answer vocally.

"Well?" she yelled, nearly jumping out of her seat.

"I got in," I said quietly. Too quietly.

"What?"

"I said, I got in."

"To which ones?" she asked, picking up her coffee mug that was in the shape of a kitten's head.

"All of them," I said.

Mrs. Schnauzer dropped the mug in her lap and let out a string of profanities that sounded very odd coming from a tiny blond woman who had just been drinking out of a kitten mug.

"I am sorry. That is so unprofessional. But, um, did you just say you got in to all of them?" she asked, not even trying to clean up the mess all over herself.

I nodded then said, "Do you want me to get a towel or something?"

As if she didn't hear me at all, she said, "Are you saying you got in to all seventeen colleges you applied to, including the eight Ivys?"

I nodded again. Mrs. Schnauzer let out another string of profanities. "I'm sorry. I am so sorry. This is very unprofessional of me." She took her chair and dragged it around to the other side of the desk so that she was sitting right in front of me. And I mean really close to me. I could practically feel the heat from the coffee that she had just spilled on her lap. "I'm just ... I just ...Why didn't you ... I don't understand why you didn't tell me about this. Do your parents know? Why are you not more excited?"

I shrugged. Mrs. Schnauzer balled her hands into fists and tapped the sides of her face as if she was trying with all her might to restrain herself. "I'm going to need you to get a little more excited about this, okay?"

"Okay," I said dutifully.

"No, no, no. Not good enough. Try again."

"Yay!" I said with a fake, exaggerated smile and a fist pump in the air.

"Well, we certainly know you didn't get in for your acting ability. Bria," she said, taking my hands in hers, "do you realize that I have been a college counselor for twenty-seven years and I have never had a student get into seventeen top tier schools? In fact, I'm going to call you Ms. Ivy because you got into all of the Ivy Leagues. I should call the news. Oh, I am definitely calling the local news. This is newsworthy. The world is your oyster, Bria Browning. You have some big decisions to make. What are you thinking? Where do you want to go? What is your first choice? Stanford? Harvard? Yale?"

I sighed. I didn't want to think about this actually. Recently, I had been avoiding thoughts of college. If I went away to college, that meant leaving Xander when I had just gotten him back.

"Maybe Johns Hopkins?" she volunteered. "It's where your dad went. Maybe you want to follow in his footsteps, huh?"

I shook my head. "Definitely not. Um, I was actually just thinking about going to the University of Colorado in Denver."

Mrs. Schnauzer squinted at me as if she couldn't quite see me. She was so confused.

"Okay, first of all, you got in to seventeen of the top twenty-five schools in the country and you want to go to University of Colorado? What? Second of all, you didn't even apply there! What is wrong with you? Sorry. I'm sorry. That was unprofessional. You're an adult. You're eighteen. You can make these decisions. It's your life." Mrs. Schnauzer stood for a moment, walked in a circle and then sat back down. "What I meant to say is, what is making you want to stay in Denver all of the sudden?"

"Xander," I said simply.

"Xander? What the hell is a Xander?" she said, having a harder and harder time hiding her frustration.

"He's not a what. He's a who. Xander Vaughn. He's my boyfriend."

Mrs. Schnauzer sighed. "Okay, I see what's going on here. This is about a boy. This is an easy fix. Does he go to this school?" After I nodded, Mrs. Schnauzer awkwardly scooted her chair around to the other side of her desk and started to type on her computer. She wouldn't be familiar with Xander as a student because she was only assigned students with last names from A-M. She would have to look up his record to find out who he was. "Let's just see what kind of student he is. Maybe you two can go to the same school and live happily ever after. Oh," she said with a combination of shock and disappointment, obviously finding his records. "Well, that's not good. Not good at all. I see you're not with him for his smarts. I'm sorry. I am so sorry. That is so unprofessional. But damn, he had to take geometry twice! Twice! Bria, what do you see in this kid? Nope, sorry. Don't answer that. I shouldn't have asked that. It's none of my business. Not professional."

"Do me a favor, Mrs. Schnauzer, and Google Xander and Kimmy Vaughn," I said.

After typing that into her computer she said, "Oh, okay, well, I see what you see in him. He is virtually a celebrity." She read a few of the Google results. "And it seems like they are on their way to being world famous. These kids go here? How did I miss this?"

"Just him. His sister is homeschooled."

"Ah, right." Mrs. Schnauzer turned away from her computer and faced me. She clasped her hands together and took another moment before she spoke, probably trying to find the most professional words she could. "So," she said carefully, "how long have you and Xander been together?"

"Four days."

"Dear God!" she said, slamming her face on her desk. I could tell I was not making a good case for my decision to stay in the Denver area.

"But this is the second time we're together," I said, feeling like I needed to explain the situation a little more.

"Last year we were together for six months and then we broke up and we got back together four days ago."

"And what if you break up again in another six months?" she asked, looking at me.

"We won't."

"Bria, I'm going to be real with you. You're eighteen. Your emotions are strong. Really strong. You feel like you're never going to feel this way again for anyone else. But let me tell you. You're only eighteen. You have a lot of life left, a lot of living to do. Please don't make a decision that will affect the rest of your life based on how you may be feeling today."

"What am I supposed to do? Leave him when I just got him back?"

She sighed. "Bria, are you smarter now than you were when you were nine years old?"

"Of course."

"Don't you think you're going to be smarter at twenty-seven years old than you are now?"

"That seems like a valid extrapolation."

"Don't make this decision for eighteen-year-old Bria. Make it for twenty-seven-year-old Bria. What would she want out of life? Where do you want to be nine years from now?"

I didn't say it out loud for fear that Mrs. Schnauzer would have another unprofessional outburst but I knew that nine years from now, all I wanted was to be Mrs. Xander Vaughn.

Chapter 13: Bria

I couldn't get my meeting with Mrs. Schnauzer out of my head. Her logic just made too much sense. How could I make decisions about my future based on my eighteen-year-old girl emotions? Wasn't I smarter than that? But no matter how much my mind told me to leave Denver to go to my first choice, Stanford, my heart was screaming at me that it wouldn't survive another break up with Xander. Just thinking about it made it hard to breathe.

I was so conflicted I couldn't even come up with a theory or a compromise. I had to talk to Xander. Of course, he wasn't in school. I knew he would be at Kimmy's side whenever possible for the foreseeable future.

`Can we talk?` I texted to him

`Of course. Talking is my second favorite thing to do with you.`

My heart fluttered. He could reduce me to a puddle just from a text message. How was I supposed to leave that? How could I not want to be near that twenty-five out of twenty-four hours a day?

We met in the cafeteria of the hospital where he had a cup of peppermint cocoa waiting for me. He hugged me tightly, clinging to me as if he needed to hold on to something. "I missed you, Bria Bear," he said after kissing me gently on the lips.

"Missed you too, Xanadu," I said. We sat down and I took a sip of cocoa.

"What's wrong?" he asked.

I didn't try to lie and make it seem like everything was fine. He knew me too well for that. He knew something was on my mind and it was worrying me. I took another sip, trying to figure out a delicate way to bring up the subject. It was such bad timing. I felt selfish for even thinking about my college career when his sister was dying right upstairs. Reaching across the table to hold my hand, he said, "You're worried. You never worry. You always have a plan."

"I don't have a plan this time," I said. "I don't even have a theory and that's what scares me."

"Tell me. Maybe I can come up with the plan for the first time ... ever."

I took a deep breath and said, "I got into every college I applied to."

Xander shrugged. "Well, of course you did, Bria. You're a genius."

"What are your college plans, Xander?" My voice was thin and wimpy. I felt so awkward asking him this. Was it really my business?

"Oh," he said, realizing my dilemma.

"Xander, I don't want to lose you when I just got you back."

He brought my hand to his lips. After kissing the back of my hand and then the inside of my wrist, he said, "You're not going to lose me. I'm not going anywhere. Literally, I'm not going anywhere. Have you seen my grades?"

I didn't want to, but I smiled. Xander put his hand on my cheek and I leaned into his hand as he cradled my face and brushed his thumb against my lips. "Bria, you can go anywhere you want to for school. This is not a bad thing. It's a good thing. It's incredible. And no matter what you decide, college is like six months away. We have time to come up with a solution."

"Three months," I corrected him.

"Three? Why?"

"I got accepted into a summer research program at Stanford. It starts in June. It's such an amazing opportunity, I can't reject it. I can't. But I also can't leave you. I don't want to be without you again."

Xander took a deep breath. He dropped my hand and ran his fingers through his dark hair. "Okay, June. Three months. That's sooner than I expected, but we'll deal. California. California's cool. I can live there. They have ice rinks, right? No biggie. I can find an apartment. We can find an apartment together ... If that's okay with you."

My eyes widened. "You would be willing to move to California for me?"

"Of course." The way he said it with no hesitation instantly made tears form behind my eyes and a lump form in my throat. He was the only thing on the planet that brought out that kind of emotion in me.

"What about Kimmy? You're a pairs skater. She'd have to move too."

Xander chewed on his thumbnail as he said, "Right, Kimmy. Didn't think of that."

"It's okay. You ... We don't have to decide anything today. The guidance counselor brought it up and I started to worry and—"

"I don't want you to worry. I don't want you to ever question how much I love you and how much I want to be with you." He stood up and then sat back down again quickly. "I'll take a break from skating," he said as if he had just come up with the most brilliant solution on the planet.

"What? That's crazy. I can't let you—"

"No, think about it. I'm a pairs skater like you said and my partner is sick. She won't be back on her feet for at least a year, right? Even if we find a donor today she's gotta go through the transplant and chemo and then get her strength back. It's gonna take time. During that time I'll just take a break. I'll give skating lessons or coach Little League hockey or something. Hell, I'll work at Burger King if I have to until it's time to start training again. We can make it work. And we can be together during that time. If that's okay. I mean, if that's what you want."

I nodded. "It's what I want."

"Okay, it's settled. We'll get an apartment in Stanford and I will make your breakfast and pack your lunch to take to your little research thing and cook you dinner when you get home and then we'll make every night November second."

My eyes grew large. "You remember."

"Of course, I do."

Chapter 14: Xander

Patrick Vaughn was not my father. Sure, he may have impregnated my mother eighteen years and nine months ago. But he was not my father. He gave up the right long ago. After how he treated Bria that night, I stopped calling him Dad. For a while, I just called him the Sperm Donor, but my mother made me stop. After trying on a few other nicknames like the Walking Dick and Ass Hat, I settled on just plain Patrick.

Our relationship began to deteriorate when I was about eight years old. That was when I decided to become a figure skater instead of a hockey player. Patrick Vaughn, professional hockey player, was not pleased. He was hoping I would follow in his ice tracks and perhaps bring validation to his mediocre career.

Patrick grew up having the best and being the best. He was the star of his high school ice hockey team and with that came fame, and girls, and college scholarships. He choose to attend Notre Dame. Not for any special reason. He probably had just seen the movie Rudy. Who knew? After a college career that was pretty good but not as stellar as high school, he was drafted to the Colorado Avalanche. He probably could have had a good career if he had focused on his game. Instead, he was too focused on drugs, alcohol, and women. He would show up to practice drunk, miss games, provide unauthorized interviews with the press and generally cause his team and owners a whole lot of trouble. After two years with the Avalanche he was traded, and then traded again, and again, and again. Three years ago, the Avalanche offered him another contract, probably out of pity, and he returned to finish out his career.

At some point, early in his career, he impregnated a Russian bartender also known as my mother Nadia. I don't know much about my mother's childhood. Just that she was extremely poor. So poor that she was never able to have the gymnastics training she had always desired.

The details on how my parents met were not PG rated apparently, because neither Kimmy nor I had ever heard the full story. I didn't know whether it was love or merely an attempt to avoid another paternity suit but for some reason, they got married. The rest was history. Well, if history involved a loveless marriage and a dysfunctional family.

I couldn't really blame Patrick for everything. Nadia was not the picture of a suburban soccer mom. She really had no idea how to be a mom or how to raise kids.

I remember once when I was about seven, I was playing in a Junior Hockey League game. At one point after I missed a goal, I looked into the crowd and saw my mom yelling at someone. The next thing I knew they were throwing punches. When the referees threw her out, she first walked out on the ice, grabbed me by the shoulder pads and dragged me away as well. It was mid-game. I never knew what the argument was about. I never found out and I never asked. It didn't matter. I was actually used to it at that point.

Even when I started figure skating, she would cause a scene so often during our competitions that she was banned from most rinks in the state. In my book, it was a bonus that our current skating club didn't appreciate her presence and only allowed her to come with advance notice. I loved being able to skate and not having to worry about her showing up and embarrassing us. She actually had little to say about our skating careers as long as we kept winning.

There were two things my parents had in common. First, was their hot tempers. They fought like they were going to murder each other and less than an hour later they would pretend like nothing had happened and start calling each other nicknames like they were in love. But it was pretty unconvincing because all Patrick could ever come up with was dear and honey. And my mom would call him some names in Russian that I was pretty sure weren't all complimentary. In any case, they tried to pretend they liked each other. It was weird, unsettling, and probably very unhealthy. Their relationship was like a sick codependency that was fed by drama and dysfunction.

The second thing my parents agreed on was that Kimmy and I needed to be extraordinary at all times. I think that's why Kimmy had it in her mind that we needed to make it to the Olympics. A part of her felt that if we were successful, it would make our parents so happy that they would stop fighting and we could be a normal family. She failed to realize that there was absolutely nothing that could make the Vaughns normal.

My home life was like navigating a minefield. Worrying about what I might say or do that would set one of them off. They never really got physical with us that often. Most of the time my dad just punched the wall or a table. Except for the time Patrick caught me with Bria. Other than that, it was really just incessant yelling and arguing. I guess I got off easy on that front. But instead of enduring the yelling and the arguing, I usually just tried to fly under the radar and avoid them. If I'm being honest, sometimes, especially in my early teens, I would try to provoke them. But then I realized I never wanted to become as angry as they did. I think that was another reason I loved Bria. She had a calming effect on me. She eased my stress and my worries instead of exacerbating them like my parents did.

I often tried to make comparisons between my parents and Bria's parents. They were so completely different. Bria seemed to think that the emotion my parents showed, though misguided, at least proved that they cared for me as opposed to her parents who would completely forget they even had a child if they didn't have to pay her credit card bill once a month.

She called it her Thin Line Theory, based on the saying "there's a thin line between love and hate." "The opposite of love isn't hate," she said to me one day. "Hating someone takes effort. It is an active emotion. You have to care enough to hate them. That hate was not too far away from love. The emotion could transfer. The opposite of love is ambivalence. And it is very difficult to learn to love something or someone that doesn't even register on your map of existence."

I knew Bria was a technical genius. I mean, like, perfect score on the SATs type of genius, but if a career as a scientist or mathematician or astronaut didn't work out, she would always make an amazing therapist or psychologist.

"If they are yelling at you," she said, "at least it means they care."

That was supposed to make me feel better. It didn't. The yelling and the fighting stressed me out beyond comprehension. I had organized my life in a way to spend as little time as possible with my parents. That wasn't healthy and it wasn't normal. But it was necessary for my survival.

Chapter 15: Xander

My distress about not being a match to Kimmy led Bria to come up with an idea. In less than a week, my brilliant Bria had been able to organize a citywide bone marrow donation drive for Kimmy. Two local television stations and three radio stations broadcast the event ensuring that a steady stream of donors flowed through our high school gym all day long.

Bria had teamed up with the Be The Match Foundation and had used her dad's connections at the hospital to get extra doctors and nurses to volunteer for the event.

In advance of the donation drive, she made sure to plaster the city with pictures of Little Kimmy Vaughn, mostly in ice skating costumes to motivate people to turn out for the event.

Bria even thought of food. She had contacted restaurants, bakeries and coffee shops to donate snacks and treats for everyone who came out. The result was an event that was solemn but not sad. Over 3,000 people came to help Kimmy, but even if they weren't a match to her, they could potentially save thousands of other people. I was absolutely overwhelmed by how hard Bria had worked on this. I could add event planning to the list of things she was amazing at. Planning a donation drive was not only something I didn't even think of, it was something that I would have been completely incapable of doing on my own. Seeing Bria in action left me utterly breathless and speechless at the same time. How could someone so remarkable love me? I was nothing compared to her. All I did was slide around ice to the beat of some music.

Since Kimmy didn't go to public school, most of the people there didn't know who she was. They had only known her as my sister and skating partner or they had just learned about her from Bria's donation campaign. But there were a few people that knew her personally, like Kimmy's ex-boyfriend Joshua Becker. Even though he was a year behind me at the same high school, I didn't know him too well. I just knew he was on the baseball team, that everyone called him Becker and that he met Kimmy one weekend at the ice skating rink. After that first meeting, I remember seeing them together for most of the summer, but by the time school was about to start they had fizzled out.

"Look it, um, tell your sister I hope she feels better," Becker said as he filled out his paperwork. He was still in his baseball uniform. Bria had arranged for all the sports teams to stop by and donate after whatever practices or games they had. She even convinced some teachers to give extra credit to those who donated. Like I said earlier, she was amazing.

"Why don't you tell her yourself?" I said. "She could use some visitors besides me and Bria."

"Yeah, I don't think she'd want to see me," he said as he rubbed the back of his neck "We didn't end well."

"Why not?" I asked.

Joshua got a panicked look on his face. "Uh, she didn't tell you?"

I thought back to last summer. I just remember Kimmy telling me that she didn't have time for a boyfriend and that he was distracting her from training. But looking at Joshua's worried expression, I got the feeling that wasn't true. There was more to this story.

"I want *you* to tell me," I said. "Why didn't you and my sister end well?" I crossed my arms menacingly and waited for his response.

"Xander, breathe," Bria said. She put her hand on my back as if to let me know she was there for me. Normally, that would have been enough to calm me down, but not after what Becker said next.

"Bro, you know how it is. I was just looking to get a little summer action and she got really clingy after we—"

He didn't get to finish that sentence. I leaped across the table and punched him in the face.

"Xander, stop!" Bria yelled. But I didn't. I got two or three more punches in before she got between us. I had to quickly jerk back my fist to avoid hitting her. I never would have forgiven myself if I had accidently punched her instead of Becker.

"You are better than this. You are not your father," she said so quietly that only I could hear her. She pushed me away from him and toward the exit. "Let me see your hand," she said once we were outside the gym. She took a napkin out of her black mini backpack and started wiping the blood off of my knuckles.

"Sorry about that," I said. "I don't know what came over me."

"I do," she said, gently squeezing each finger on my now injured hand. "Your only sister is dying. You're stressed out. You want to hit something and Joshua Becker has a very punchable face."

I smiled at her. How could she be so calm and forgiving when I could have just ruined the event she had worked so hard to prepare for my sister?

"I think your hand is fine," she said. "Nothing broken. And the blood is not from you, Xanadu."

"Thanks, Bria Bear. I don't know what I would do without you right now." I leaned down to kiss her.

"Oh, gross!" someone said.

I turned to see Heidi Hopley sneering at us. How did this day suddenly turn into a parade of jackasses?

Bria sighed, looked at Heidi and started reciting numbers.

"Shows how much you know," Heidi said, interrupting her. "I changed my credit card. I have a new number."

"And you used it yesterday when you bought prom tickets for you and your loser college boyfriend. What was his name again? Tad? Brad?"

"Chad," Heidi corrected.

"Whatever. Anyway, when you bought the tickets, I saw the number plain as day. I repeat 4178—"

"Shut up!" Heidi yelled. "You are such a freak!"

"OMG, Heidi you're going to have to get a new credit card again," her friend said. "Your dad's gonna be so pissed."

"Shut up, Kellan!" Heidi stormed off in the opposite direction of the gym. If she wasn't going to donate, why was she even there on a Saturday? It wasn't like she had practice for a team or something. The girl literally did nothing.

"How do you keep doing that, Bria?" I asked. "I mean, I know you're great at memorizing numbers but how do you keep getting such good looks at her credit card?"

Bria shrugged. "I don't. I have no idea what her credit card number is, but obviously, neither does she."

Chapter 16: Bria

"Should I confront her about it?" Xander asked me after the donor drive as we were on our way to the hospital. The donor drive that was a huge success if I did say so myself. I just hoped it was enough. Of the 3,000 people that showed up to help Kimmy, at least one of them had to be a match, right? Statistically speaking.

"Confront who about what?" I asked.

Xander stopped at a red light and looked at me as if I had two heads. "Kimmy about Becker."

"Why on Earth would you do that?"

"She's my little sister and I don't like the idea of a guy taking advantage of her."

"Xander, you can't be serious." Just then the car behind us honked. We both looked forward and saw that the light had changed.

"Why wouldn't I be serious?" he said as he drove on.

"This is perhaps the most insane thing you have ever said to me in your life and that includes when you tried to tell me that Rihanna is the greatest singer of our time."

"Hey, don't hate on Ri-Ri!"

"Her voice is the human equivalent of a cheese grater," I said.

"You know, we are just going to have to agree to disagree on that," he said, feigning anger.

"Whatever. It's a free country. You have a right to be wrong."

"Except I'm not. And just so you know, we are totally dancing to Rihanna at our wedding. I can see "Stay" as our first dance as husband and wife."

"Alexander Dmitri Vaughn, I swear to God if you play Rihanna at our wedding I will divorce you immediately!" I was only half joking. I mean I really did hate Rihanna and didn't understand what he saw in her, but I did kind of like our faux arguments about her. "And you know what? Any sane judge will rule in my favor and force you to pay me for the emotional damage caused by actually having to listen to Rihanna."

"You know you kind of look like her, right?" he said. "Is that why you don't like her? Are you jealous? Don't worry; I can love you both!"

I punched him in the arm as hard as I could which wasn't very, but he still pretended like I had shot him or something. "Compare her to me again and we are through, Xanadu. Finished. I will never marry you for as long as we both shall live."

We both paused for a moment realizing that we had just referred to our wedding as if it were a real thing that we had planned and was about to happen any moment.

"Anyway," he said finally, "why is it insane? The Becker thing. I want to find out why she didn't tell me."

"First of all, no sixteen-year-old girl wants to talk about her sex life with her big brother."

"That's just it. She's only sixteen. She shouldn't have a sex life."

"Did you say that about me when I was sixteen?"

"That's different. You're not my sister."

"I'll rephrase. Did you say it about yourself when you were sixteen?"

"No," he admitted sheepishly.

"Double standard much?"

Xander nodded in acceptance. "That's fair," he said as he pulled into the hospital parking lot.

"Second of all," I said as he turned off the car. He leaned his head back on the headrest and stared at me. "Becker obviously hurt her so much she was too ashamed to bring it up to you. You. The most important person in her world. What makes you think she wants to bring up that kind of pain now that she's in the hospital battling aplastic anemia?"

"You know what's most remarkable about you?" he said, somewhat off topic. "You're not only book smart, you're emotionally smart. That's an extremely rare combination."

"You are no so bad yourself, Xander Vaughn," I said before kissing him.

"What should I do, Bria?" he asked.

"I have an idea."

Two hours later, we were sitting in Kimmy's room watching Jeopardy and eating pizza.

"You should go on this show, Bria," Kimmy said.

"Eh, not my thing," I said. "I don't like being in front of all those people. There's a live studio audience, you know. I'd probably poop my pants. I don't know how you and Xander do it all the time."

"Ah, it's such a rush. I love it!" Kimmy said. "And though Xan probably won't admit it, he loves it too."

Xander simultaneously shrugged and nodded. "Yeah, I do kind of like it. Maybe I can give you some pointers, Bria."

"Why? Pointers for what?"

Kimmy and Xander exchanged a glance. "What do you mean why? You know you're going to have to give the valedictorian speech, right?"

Holy smokes. He was right. I would have to give a speech. And our school had over 2,000 students. There were 449 graduating seniors. Each of them would be there along with their parents, and maybe grandparents, and siblings, and aunts and uncles. Maybe even some cousins in attendance. And then faculty as well. I would have to give a speech in front of thousands. Thousands!

"Bria, Bria, you okay?" Xander said, squeezing my hand.

"What? Yeah, why?" I asked.

"Because you haven't said anything in five minutes. You've just been staring straight ahead like you're ... Bria, are you scared of giving a little graduation speech?"

"Little?" I asked. "By my calculations there will be at least 3,000 people there."

"So?" Kimmy said.

"Maybe I won't have to give the speech. You know, Steven Portman's GPA is really close to mine. Maybe he'll catch me before the end of the school year."

"I know you're better at numbers than I am, but I'm pretty sure you could flunk all of your classes for the rest of the year and you'd still have the highest GPA by far," Xander said.

"Well, maybe I'll just pass on giving the speech. Or maybe I will lose my voice. They can't make me give a speech. Can they? Oh my God, can they make it mandatory?"

"Dude, why are you so freaked out about this?" Kimmy asked. "You're good at everything. You'll be great at giving a speech."

"Yeah, just pretend the audience is full of Heidi Hopleys."

Kimmy squealed. "OMG! Was there another Heidi incident? Tell me everything."

We told her what happened with Heidi including the fact that I really didn't know her credit card number and Kimmy laughed like crazy. "You made her think you knew her credit card number, not once but twice! She's such an idiot."

Once our laughter subsided a little, Xander looked at me. I gave a slight nod of approval and he said, "We also saw Josh Becker." Kimmy stared at her brother but didn't say anything. "I punched him in the face. I think I broke his nose."

Kimmy nodded slowly. "Cool."

And that was the last time either of us ever mentioned Joshua Becker.

Moments later, two of Kimmy's friends from their skating club came by. Xander and I left them to hang out and took this opportunity to have some alone time. He thought it was about time we had a real date but we had just eaten and I hated the idea of movie theater dates. You couldn't really talk to a person if you were in a movie theater; it was kind of frowned upon. I think we were both too tired to think of some sort of crazy romantic outing. There really wasn't much for us to do. Thus, we opted for a walk through City Park.

"This is nice, right?" he said, squeezing my hand.

"What's nice?" I asked even though I knew exactly what he was talking about.

"This. Us. Being together."

"Yeah," I said with a big goofy grin. "We've been back together for only two weeks and it feels like we were never apart."

"I know, right? I'm glad I'm not the only one who feels that." Xander looked away nervously and stuffed his free hand into his pocket.

"What's wrong?" I asked.

"Nothing."

"Xander." I stopped walking and turned to him. "Hey, just tell me what's up."

Looking around briefly, he spotted an empty bench and pulled me over to it. After sitting down, he took both my hands in his and said, "I want to continue talking about what we were talking about earlier today."

Somehow, I knew exactly what he meant even though his statement sounded vague and insane.

"The wedding thing?" I asked.

"Yeah. I mean, I know it's crazy and we've only been back together for two weeks and we're only eighteen, but didn't the whole idea sound—"

"Normal," I said.

"Yes! Exactly. How can something that on the surface seems completely and utterly insane feel so completely natural?"

"So what does that mean?" I asked. I was actually surprised I could speak; my heart was beating so fast.

"I think you know what it means," he said.

I shot up off the bench and started pacing in front of him. "Xander, we can't get married. There's too much to think about. There has to be a plan. When would it happen? Where would we live? What about college? How are we going to pay rent?"

"What does it matter so long as we're together?"

"You know it matters. This is not how I operate. I ... I need a plan. I need to do research and make sure things will at least work on paper."

Xander grabbed my hand, pulled me to him and kissed me probably just to shut me up. I was starting to get a little frantic.

"I promise I will let you do all the research and planning you need to do," he said when he let me up for air. "Just promise me two things, right here and right now."

"Okay," I whispered breathlessly. In that moment I would have promised him anything. My mind was complete mush.

"First, promise me you will marry me one day."

I took a deep breath and said, "I promise." I wanted to scream. I was going to marry Alexander Vaughn! How was this even possible?

Xander had the biggest smile I had ever seen on his face which made me smile which made us both start giggling like idiots.

"What's the second thing?" I asked.

"Oh, right." His genuinely happy smile morphed into a devilish grin as he said, "Promise me that we can do our first dance to a Rihanna song."

Chapter 17: Xander

"I have good news," Dr. Givens, the specialist, said Monday morning. "We found a usable match."

"Already?" my mom said, coming to her feet. "Wasn't that fast?'

"We need fast," he said. "I'm not going to lie: Kimbra is in a very dire situation. I have not seen someone deteriorate so quickly. We had to fast track the donations. If we wait any longer—"

"Who's the match?" Patrick asked, interrupting the doctor. "Is it a perfect match? Is there a chance her body will reject it like she did the blood transfusion?"

"No, it is not a perfect match," Dr. Givens admitted. "So, yes, there is always the chance that her body will reject it, but there is a clinical trial happening for haploidentical matches that I think Kimbra will do well in. There are a series of treatments she needs to go through beforehand that will help ensure that her body will accept the match. We are going to start her on those right now."

"What kind of treatments?" I asked, watching Nurse James change Kimmy's IV bag. "And what is a haploidentical match?"

"We basically need to completely destroy Kimbra's immune system. She won't be able to leave the hospital for at least six weeks," the Doctor said. "And a haploidentical match means that the donor is a half match.

It seems to be as close as we're going to get. Kimbra's genetic makeup is ... unique."

Unique? What did he mean by that?

"In any case, it is very fortunate that you and your friends threw that donation drive. The matching donor was found through that."

"One of Xander's friends is going to save my life?" Kimmy asked. "Who is it?"

"Legally, I can't tell you that." Then he smiled. "But I have a feeling she will tell you all herself."

What did that mean? I thought. But then my phone buzzed. It was a text from Bria that said,

```
I'm a match!
```

I was so confused. How was it possible that Bria was a better match to Kimmy than me? I mean, I was her brother. And how random was it that a non-related match happened to not only show up in our own city but be my girlfriend?

I stepped into the hallway and gave her a call.

"I'm a match!" she said when she answered the phone.

"That's amazing! I'm so happy I could cry." That was a lie since I was actually already crying at the time. "You're gonna save Kimmy's life."

"Well, I hope so. I'm not a perfect match."

"You're the best we've got. It's gonna work. It has to. Where are you?"

"I'm skipping school and heading to the hospital. They want me to donate as soon as possible so why not now?"

"God, I love you so much, Bria. You have no idea."

"I love you too."

I wasn't sure what a donation involved but I assumed it would be painful and/or uncomfortable. Bria was going to go through all this pain just to save my sister. I wanted, no, I needed to do something special for her. Not wanting to go too far from the hospital, I raided the gift store and bought flowers, candy, and a Rubik's Cube. I figured that could keep her busy for at least a few minutes. Then I waited outside the room they had set aside for Bria. She arrived a few minutes later.

"I got these for you," I said, holding out my gifts.

"You didn't have to do that," she said, kissing me on the cheek.

"Of course, I did." I couldn't believe this was happening. Soon my girlfriend's blood would be running through my sister's veins. Okay, it was weird to think of it that way. "Do your parents know you're here? Do they know what you're about to do?"

"For one thing, they wouldn't care. For another thing, I'm eighteen so I don't have to tell them. Besides, this will be a quick procedure. I'll be under for less than an hour and then, I'll let you take me home." She smiled and kissed me.

Bria was right about one thing. It was a quick procedure. She was back in her hospital room minutes later. I sat and watched her sleep for a while. She was so peaceful and beautiful. Almost immediately after we met I had gotten the impression that she didn't think she was attractive. She seemed resigned to that fact even though I had no idea why she would feel that way. Honestly, she reminded me of a more understated and classically beautiful version of Rihanna. Kind of like if Rihanna was a comic book nerd if that made any sense. In any case, the comparison helped fuel my borderline fascination with the admittedly mediocre pop singer.

Bria's insecurities probably came from her parents. On paper and in pictures, the Brownings were the essence of perfection. In fact, they had even made Couple of the Year or something for Essence magazine. Dr. Browning was a world-renowned pediatrician who looked like a grown-up version of Steph Curry and Mrs. Browning was a former model who looked like a tall Angela Bassett. It was a lot for a teenage girl to live up to. And her parents had done a horrible job of making her feel wanted or worthwhile. That was why I told her she was beautiful every chance I got.

Wow, we had both gotten shafted in the whole parent lottery. Maybe that was another reason why we were so connected. We each knew what it was like to be lacking in the parental arena. I wasn't going to let our unfortunate upbringing stand in the way of our future happiness, however. It would be Bria and I against the world.

An hour later, she was already awake and I was sitting right next to her bed.

"How are you feeling?" I asked her.

"Good, not great."

"Well, you look amazing. This fluorescent white gown really suits you."

Bria started to laugh and then winced in pain. "How's Kimmy?" she asked.

"Let's just focus on you for now," I said, not wanting to worry her. Thankfully, a nurse came in to take her vitals, preventing her from asking any more questions about Kimmy.

"Is everything okay," I asked the nurse when I noticed she was taking a while.

The nurse glanced at Bria. "It's okay, he's my boyfriend," she said, squeezing my hand.

"Your temperature is slightly elevated and your blood pressure is a little low. I think we should keep you for observation for a few hours."

"What does that mean?" I asked. "Is everything okay?"

"I'm sure she's fine."

But she wasn't fine. Apparently, Bria had developed an infection and they wouldn't release her.

Around five that evening, Bria's father, Dr. Browning showed up while she was sleeping. "What's going on here?" he asked as he grabbed her chart and started reading it himself.

"Hi, um, Bria just donated blood marrow," I said.

"What? Why wasn't I told? She needs my approval."

I shook my head. "She's eighteen." *Did you honestly forget her birthday?* I thought. What a piece of work.

"Damn it, she has a staph infection at the donation site in her hip. She could die from trying to save someone else's life."

He said it so coldly. Even if he didn't realize that the life she was trying to save was my sister's, you would think his own daughter's mortality would cause him to have a little compassion. "Why is she even donating marrow? I didn't even know she was on the registry," he said.

Yeah, there's a lot you don't know about her, I thought.

"Why are you here?" he asked. I thought about telling him that Bria and I were a couple again, but I didn't feel like dealing with that. Instead, I said, "The recipient is my sister, Kimmy."

Dr. Browning looked up from the chart. "Bria was a match for your sister?"

"Yes."

Immediately, he closed the chart and stormed out of the room.

~~~

I wanted to sit by the bedside of both Kimmy and Bria. But I could only be in one place at a time unfortunately. And since my parents were with Kimmy, I stayed with Bria. I didn't want to be around my parents anyway. Plus, Bria had no one. Her dad was on call in the hospital and her mother was in Germany for a fundraiser. So, there was just me. We hadn't really had a chance to sit down and talk about what was happening. It all went so fast. I should have asked more questions. I should have been aware of the side effects and possible complications. But everyone sounded so sure, so positive, so convinced that donating marrow was a simple, quick and easy procedure. But that was the same thing they had said about Kimmy's blood transfusion two weeks ago and look how that turned out. I felt like every girl I cared about in my life was doomed to suffer right in front of me. Why wasn't it me? Why wasn't I the one to get sick? Why wasn't I the one who was able to save my sister with a marrow donation?

Bria slept continuously for nine hours straight. Every hour or so I would go check on Kim to see how she was doing. Kim assured me she was fine even though she looked pale, weak and like she had just finished puking every time I saw her. Probably because she had just puked. Her doctors were essentially poisoning her so that her body wouldn't be able to fight against the bone marrow donation that Bria was about to give her.

"I'm fine, Xan, seriously," she said to me around midnight. "Mom's here. She can take care of me. You go be with Bria; she needs you more." I wanted to kiss her on the forehead, but the doctors advised against physical contact. Kimmy would basically have no immune system for the next few weeks and they thought it best to avoid possible germ transference.

So I just went back to Bria. And it was a good thing I did because for the first time in like twelve hours, she actually woke up.

"Where am I?" she asked, confused.

"You're in the hospital."

"Why?"

Oh God, I thought. Did she lose her memory?

"You donated bone marrow to Kimmy. Don't you remember?"

"Yes, I remember that. But why am I a match to her? That is statistically improbable. And why am I still here in the hospital?"

"You got an infection at the donation site. You can't leave until it's cleared up, I think."

Bria looked at the clock on the wall. "Is that time right? Have I been here all day?"

I nodded. "This is ridiculous. I'm fine," she said, whipping off the sheets and trying to stand.

"Bria, please lie back down. They wouldn't want you to stay if it wasn't necessary." I grabbed her arms to try to gently maneuver her back to the bed and that was when I noticed how hot her skin was to the touch. Suddenly, her eyes rolled to the back of her head and she started shaking violently.

"Somebody help!" I yelled.

Instantly, a team of doctors and nurses burst into the room.

"She's seizing," someone said.

"Get Dr. Browning down here," someone else said.

"You're going to have to leave," yet another person said. It took me a moment to realize that person was talking to me.

"What's happening? What's wrong with her?" I asked as they pushed me out of the room.

Seconds later, Bria's father came rushing past me.

"What's going on?" I yelled, but he ignored me and went into the hospital room.

"Who's in surgery right now?" I heard him ask. "It's spreading. We need to operate."

Operate? Why would they need to put her back in surgery?

As they wheeled her out of the room, I grabbed Dr. Browning and asked, "Can you please tell me what's going on? Is she going to be all right?"

Bria's father paused and said, "Don't worry. We've tested the donation and it's clean. Your sister won't be affected."

"But what about Bria? Is she going to be okay?"

"Why do you care?"

"Because I ... I love her."

"Great. That's just what we need right now," he said before following his daughter's bed to the elevator. I could tell his tone was sarcastic but I couldn't figure out why. And who was this 'we' he was referring to?

I didn't want to be alone at that moment. I couldn't be. I went up to Kimmy's room in the oncology wing. My parents had left for the evening. Fortunately, Kimmy was awake and seemed willing to talk.

"What's wrong, Xan? You look awful," she said.

Normally, I would have made a joke about her looking worse, but it wasn't the time. I was too concerned about Bria. Plus, Kimmy was probably self-conscious about her looks at the moment.

"Bria had to go back into surgery," I said, sitting at the foot of her bed.

"Oh my God! Why?"

"Apparently she caught some sort of infection at the donation site and its spreading."

Tears started streaming down Kimmy's face. "What if she dies because of me?"

I was such an idiot. Why would I tell her what was going on with Bria? "I'm sorry, princess. I shouldn't have burdened you with this. She is going to be fine. Her dad said so himself and he said the sample is clean. You are going to get healthy and Bria is going to be fine as well."

Kimmy shook her head. "You don't know that. No one knows anything. Two weeks ago I was perfectly healthy and training to take Nationals. Now my life depends on a transplant from my brother's girlfriend and I may never skate again."

"Don't say that."

"Promise me you won't stop skating," she said almost frantically. "I want you to promise me that you will go back to the rink tomorrow morning and start training."

"I promise I won't stop skating but there is no way I'm training without you. We're a team."

"No, no. You don't need me. You're better than me. You always have been. You need to start your solo career once and for all. Go to the Olympics without me."

"Kimmy, I—"

"Promise me, Xan."

"I promise."

Chapter 18: Bria

I woke up in excruciating pain. It was a pain I had never felt before. I was a bit confused for a while. The last thing I remembered was checking into the hospital to give a bone marrow donation. Yes, I was a match to Kimmy. I still didn't have time to process that information. It made no sense. I mean genetics were strange, I understood that, but for me, a black girl, to be a match to Kimmy, it just didn't make sense. The probability of that happening by chance was astronomical.

"There she is," a male voice said. I looked up and saw Nurse James standing over me. Why was he even here? He was Kimmy's nurse. This was the wrong side of the hospital. "Welcome back," he said. "I'm gonna check your vitals and then I'll get your dad."

"Okay," I said, not completely understanding what was happening.

"She's all yours," he said.

"Thanks, man," a familiar voice said. It was Xander.

"Thank God you're awake," he said, grabbing my hand. I turned my head to look at him just in time for him to kiss me on the forehead. "I was so worried."

"Why? What happened? How is Kimmy?"

"She's all right."

"Did the donation work? Is she getting better?"

Xander tucked a strand of my curly hair behind my ear. "Don't worry about her right now. You need to get better." Xander sniffled and rubbed wetness away from his eyes. Had he been crying?

"Get better? Why? What's wrong with me?" I asked. Something strange was going on.

"You don't remember anything?"

I tried to shake my head no, but everything in my body ached.

"What is the last thing you remember?"

"Just coming to the hospital to donate marrow."

"You don't remember flipping out on me and trying to walk out on your own?"

"I did no such thing," I protested but honestly, I couldn't be sure of that.

Xander smiled then entwined our fingers and kissed the back of my hand. "You caught an infection during the procedure. Your fever spiked. I think that was when you got all crazy."

"Why does my hip hurt so much?"

Xander took a deep breath. "They had to cut out a large portion of skin, muscle, and ... and bone in order to keep the infection from spreading."

"They cut my hip bone? Can I walk?" I asked, trying to hide my panic.

"Yes, they cut out part of your bone and no, you will not be able to walk at first ... It might take some time. But the good news is that they got all of it. You are completely fine. You're gonna live."

"Live? I was in danger of dying?"

I could tell by the tears that immediately welled in his eyes that I had been rather close to dying.

"How's Kimmy?" I asked again.

"They had to delay the transfusion for a day in order to make sure that the marrow was clean. But they gave it to her two days ago and so far, no reaction. Her body accepted it and she's gonna be just fine."

I loved how optimistic he was trying to be. This had been an extremely taxing few hours ... days ... Truth be told, I had no idea how long I had been there.

"Wait. Two days ago? They did the transplant two days ago? How long have I been here? Do my parents know where I am?"

"Your dad has been checking on your regularly. He is the one that ordered your surgery actually. Your mom is already on a plane back from Germany."

"Seriously? She's actually changing her plans for me?"

Xander nodded. "Yeah, she should be here any minute."

"You didn't answer my other question," I said. "How long have I been here?"

He sighed. "You've been in and out of consciousness for three days."

"Three days?" I'd been in the hospital for three days? Was it wrong that the first thing I thought of was the fact that I had a chemistry project that was now overdue? Damn, I was such a nerd.

"I'm not gonna lie, Bria. Things got pretty scary." His voice cracked and he paused to keep himself from crying. "Your fever was so high that they put you in a drug-induced coma to keep you from seizing. That's why Nurse James was here. He got himself put on your floor so he could sneak me when it was time to wake you up." Xander paused, took a deep breath and let it out slowly. "Bree. I thought ... I thought ... " A tear streamed down his face. I couldn't imagine the pain he had been through. His sister and his girlfriend in danger of dying at the same time. I had no idea how he had been able to deal. How did he even decide whose bed to sit beside? When was the last time he slept?

The sight of him crying broke my heart. "Xander. Xander, look at me," I said, cradling his face in my hands. He hadn't shaved in days and looked completely disheveled but he was still so beautiful. "I'm okay, Xander. I'm okay." I wasn't really sure if I was or not, but it was what he needed to hear. I couldn't handle seeing him like this. "Kiss me," I said, trying to distract him from his pain. He quickly obliged.

"I love you, Bria Bear," he said, resting his forehead on mine.

"I love you too, Xanadu. Now go be with your sister."

"What?"

"She needs you too. More than I do. I just had an infection that they cut out of me, right? Now they'll probably pump me full of antibiotics and I'll be fine. Kimmy just had a complete bone marrow transplant. She's in real danger. She needs you."

"But I don't want to leave you alone."

"You said my mother would be here any minute. You know how much I love her company. I'll be fine."

Xander smiled at my sarcastic lie. "Let me hold you for a little while and then I'll go."

I scooted over in the bed as he crawled in and wrapped me in his arms. In about thirty seconds, he was fast asleep.

To be honest, I didn't completely believe that my mother was going to show up. I could not remember a single time in my entire life when my mother changed her plans because of me. When I was eleven, I broke my arm while I was at school. My mother, however, was scheduled to give a speech to the United Black Business Owners of Denver. The school called her an hour before her speech. Instead of leaving immediately to comfort me or take care of me, she went on with her speech as well as the obligatory networking afterwards. She didn't show up until after I was already home and in my splint.

Then again, I had already been in the hospital for three days. Which meant it took her three days to decide to hop on a plane to see her only daughter who had almost died. Part of me wanted her here. Part of me wanted to just straight up ask her if she even remotely loved me. But then the other part of me, the sane part, was too afraid to find out the truth. Because the true answer was probably one I didn't want to know.

"Why is he in your bed?" my dad asked a few minutes later.

"He's tired. He probably hasn't slept in days."

"Well he needs to move so I can examine you," he said, picking up my chart.

"No," I said defiantly.

"Excuse me?" He was just as surprised as I was at my response. I never defied either of my parents. Probably because I never had to. They never asked me to do anything.

"He needs to sleep. I'm not waking him up. Whatever you need to do, you can do it with him lying next to me."

He sighed. "God, you're just as stubborn as your mother." He took out his stethoscope and checked my heart and my breathing before proceeding with the rest of my exam all the while working around a sleeping Xander.

"Your mother is on the way," he whispered as he flashed a light in my eyes.

"You don't have to whisper. He sleeps like … like … like someone in a drug-induced coma," I said, using a painfully appropriate analogy. "And he already told me she's flying in from Germany today."

There was a moment of silence where I wanted my father to just treat me like his child. Give me a hug and tell me everything was going to be okay. I wanted him to tell me that he loved me and that he was worried about me and that he was happy I was better. I wanted him to ask me what college I had chosen and not because he needed to factor in my college tuition into his finances. I wanted him to wonder if I was dating and if the guy was nice and if he loved me. Why couldn't he just be a father to me?

"Xander is a good kid," he said finally. "Always has been oddly enough." I was stunned into silence. I was totally not expecting that. He had an opinion on my relationship?

"You're okay with us being together?" I asked, speaking slowly. I think I was mentally keeping count of the number of words I said to my father. I think I had already passed my record for the year.

"Why wouldn't I be?" he asked.

Now I felt like I was crazy. Sure, I had a nagging doubt, a nagging suspicion about a possible genetic connection to the Vaughn family since I was a genetic match to Kimmy. But if that suspicion was correct, would my father be giving me the green light to date Xander? Unless, my father was trying some sort of reverse psychology. Or maybe, Xander and I were related but not through him and he didn't know anything about it. I was so confused.

I started making calculations in my mind. Estimating probabilities. What were the odds? What were the chances that I would be a genetic match to Kimmy Vaughn and not be related to them? I mean there was a chance, I supposed.

"I love him," I said, trying to evoke a reaction. Something I could use to refine my calculations.

"You're a little young to be in love," was his only response as he wrote something down on my chart. "Might be the pain medication."

"It's not the pain medication." I wanted to say It's not the pain medication, *Dad*, but it didn't feel sincere. I was starting to feel like how Xander felt about his father. I felt like calling him Jeffrey instead of Dad. I decided to do neither.

"Well, then it's just hormones," he said as he turned to walk out of my room.

"How dare you?" I asked indignantly.

"What?"

"You don't know anything about me or my feelings. You've never tried, you've never cared and you've never cared to try."

"Bria, what—"

"Honestly, I'm surprised you're even here. I guess almost dying is the only thing that could get you to stay in the same room with me for more than five minutes."

"What are you talking about?"

"Of course, you are a doctor at this hospital, so technically you are on the clock. Your being here doesn't even count as caring about me because you're getting paid to do it."

"That's not fair, Bria. I have always taken care of you. Good care of you. You have never wanted for anything."

"Giving me a credit card on my twelfth birthday doesn't exactly absolve you of parental duties."

Jeffrey Browning stared at me for a long time. "You're right," he said finally. "I haven't been the best father."

Yeah, I totally wasn't expecting that response either. I honestly didn't know what to say.

"You were always such a strong, independent kid. You always knew what you wanted to do. You took care of things on your own. After a while it felt like this parenting gig was on autopilot." He put down my chart and sat on the end of my bed. "But then when I saw you in here

... " He paused and cleared his throat. "You don't want to know how close we were to losing you. The surgery to remove the infection ... " He paused again. "Bria, I know I am not winning any Dad of the Year awards. I know you deserve better. I don't know if I can be better, but I will try."

"Okay," I said weakly. I hated being this weak. For years, I had planned what I would say to him in this situation. I had thought about how I would tell him off, tell him what a horrible person he was. But in the moment, I couldn't. He hadn't told me exactly what I wanted hear. He didn't say that he loved me. But he was honest. I couldn't ask for more. Besides, it was better than what my mother was about to say to me.

Chapter 19: Bria

Xander slept next to me for almost two hours. Just a few minutes after he left to check on Kimmy, my cosmopolitan mother breezed in.

"Wow, you look … good," were her first words to me in my hospital room. Was that a compliment? Or was she just surprised to see I wasn't a corpse?

"Um, thanks?"

She smiled. It wasn't a real smile. It was the exact same smile she gave to photographers after announcing the dollar amount she was donating after her latest fundraiser. "That came out wrong. What I mean is that you look a lot better than I expected when your father called saying you had some sort of deadly infection. I was literally expecting leprosy-like boils or festering cysts or something." She had an affected accent. Whenever she traveled to Europe, she came back sounding British for at least a week. It was ridiculous. She was born in Wisconsin.

"Oh, no. It was an internal infection. They had to cut out part of my hip bone."

"Internal infection," she repeated. Her eyes rolled toward the ceiling as if in thought. "An internal infection doesn't play as well for the cameras," she said more to herself than to me. "But if part of your hip bone was cut away, that should affect how you walk, correct? That would look really good on camera."

"Camera? What are you talking about?"

She looked at me confused. "Your father didn't tell you?

"Tell me what?"

"I'm running for city council. I decided to announce my candidacy today with a press conference but then cancel because of my daughter's health only to carry on with the presser after your encouragement of course."

"Why would I encourage you to—"

"Oh Ambria, don't be difficult. You know how this works. It's all about perception and appearances. And my only daughter nearly losing her life in order to save the life of another through a bone marrow donation ... God, you couldn't write better PR than that if you tried. And believe me, I've tried."

"You have got to be kidding me."

"Whatever do you mean?"

"I am in the hospital and you can't even pretend to care about my feelings or my health for even a moment. It is all about you. It's always all about you."

"Ambria, don't be dramatic. Don't you think I'd make a fantastic councilwoman?"

"You are out of your mind if you think I will help you with this."

She looked shocked. "Why not?"

"Why not? You really don't understand why I wouldn't want to endorse you?"

My mother was perhaps the most beautiful, most intelligent, and most talented person I had ever met in my life. Not only did she do a little modeling in college, but she also graduated top of her class at Duke and went on to medical school at Johns Hopkins. That's where she met my dad. Given that she was a tall, drop-dead gorgeous med student, of course my dad fell for her. They got married right before my dad started residency and I guess the rest was history. My mother left medical school to be a wife and mother.

In addition to her impressive resume, she was rather charming and manipulative, making it extremely difficult to hate her. Difficult, but not impossible. I wouldn't be surprised if by the end of our conversation I was canvassing the hospital collecting signatures for her candidacy. She just had this way of turning a conversation around on me so that by the end of it, I felt bad for her and completely forgot my own grievances. But I was determined to not let that happen this time.

"I simply don't understand why you wouldn't want to help your mother with this effort," she asked me after staring at me strangely for a while. Seriously, she couldn't understand why I wouldn't want to help her? "After all I do for you, you'd think you'd be a little grateful."

I pressed my eyes shut and tried to remain calm. Getting upset would not be helpful and could even delay my recovery. God forbid I jerked to the left or the right too hard and ripped my stiches, allowing new bacteria to enter and causing yet another infection. "And what exactly have you done for me?"

"I flew you and all your friends to Disneyland for the day for your birthday," she said with a smirk as if she had just proved her point.

"That was six years ago," I said.

"That can't be right," she said. "I distinctly remember it being your 12th birthday."

"I'm eighteen."

My mother opened her mouth to protest and realized she couldn't. She thought for a moment then said, "I named a charity after you." She was so pleased with herself she smiled, genuinely this time. I could see it in her dark eyes.

I sighed. "A. It wasn't a charity, it was a race. B. It happened when I was five. C. How is naming a race after me actually doing something for me? D. It was named the Browning 5k for Muscular Dystrophy, which is E. rather unimaginative and F. cannot really be considered named after me since there are multiple people named Browning even right here in his room."

Her smile waned. "Well, I see you have thought a lot about this."

"Incorrect again, Mother. I used to think a lot about this. I used to let it keep me up at night. I used to occupy my mind with thoughts of what I could do to make me worthy of your attention. I knew I would never be pretty enough so I tried to be smart enough. I studied constantly. Memorized facts about history, literature, and science. I studied myself into being a math whiz. I dominated the chess team, the math team, and the quiz bowl team trying to collect accomplishments that would bring your recognition, but all to no avail."

Annette Mitchell Browning was stunned into silence so I continued. "I gave up thinking about it and you and Jeffrey. I gave up on having loving parents and I found love somewhere else."

My mother cleared her throat and pretended to be in complete control as she said, "I had no idea you thought I was such a monster." She adjusted her coat as if she was about to leave and said, "I might have unwittingly and unintentionally acted like a monster over the past few years but I can assure you there is more to the story."

"Story? What story?" My mother looked prepared to bolt out the door. "What do you need to tell me?" I asked. I wanted to ask 'Why don't you love me?' but I thought that would be a little too desperate.

"You know," she began, inching her way to the door, "life isn't always black and white, little girl. There are gray areas. Things get complicated and ... messy. Maybe you should consider the possibility that you do not know the full story and thus may be ill-informed to pass judgment."

"What's the full story?" I asked. But she was already out of the door.

Chapter 20: Xander

On my way to Bria's room the next day, I saw something rather strange. Annette Browning. It was odd to see her in real life and not in a TV commercial or on the news. But what was even odder was that she was talking to my dad. What on earth could they have to talk about? I would have stared at them for a while and perhaps tried to even eavesdrop a little, but I heard something fall in Bria's room.

"What are you doing?" I yelled when I entered her room. She was shuffling around the room trying to walk well before she should have been.

"I'm fine, Xander," she said stubbornly. "I just knocked over a lamp."

"You're not fine. You just had surgery."

"I have to keep moving if I ever expect to get out of here."

"Bria, please. Sit down. You're going to hurt yourself." I took her hand and tried to lead her back to the bed.

"Xander, I'm going crazy," she said, relinquishing my hand. "I don't think I have ever sat this still before in my life. I'm bored. I have nothing to do. And for some reason, my dad keeps coming in here every two hours."

"For some reason? Bria, he's worried about you. Isn't this what you always wanted? He's showing he cares."

"Yes, he does care," she said but without the emotion or enthusiasm I was expecting. "He cares about his patient, not his daughter."

I folded her into my arms. "Bria Bear," I whispered into her hair after kissing the top of her head, "I know this is hard. I have no idea why any of this is happening to you ... to us. But we're going to get through it, okay?"

She looked up at me with tears in her eyes and said, "Are we?"

"Okay, that's it. No more of this," I said, taking her hand again and leading her to the bed. "I need you to lie down, take a nap and I will be back in less than an hour."

"Where are you going? What are you going to do?" she asked, grimacing as she crawled into bed.

"Something I should have done a long time ago," I said. "Where are your keys?"

I left the hospital with the perfect plan in mind. First, I was gonna go home, take a shower and shave. That alone would make me feel better and put me in a better position to cheer up both Kimmy and Bria. Plus, I wouldn't reek when I hugged them which I was sure they would appreciate. Then I was going to email her teachers and ask what work she needed to make up and then head to her house and pick up her schoolbooks. I know it seemed crazy, but doing schoolwork would actually make Bria feel sane again. She felt lost if she didn't have a task to do or a problem to solve. If I had time, I would also stop to buy her a puzzle. It was the perfect plan. And to be honest, I probably needed to get out of the hospital for a little while. I had been there for five days straight.

I had already gotten cleaned up at my place and was on my way to the Browning house. But when I got there, I noticed something strange. Patrick Vaughn's car. Why was my father's car in the driveway of the Browning house? Were they continuing the conversation they had started at the hospital? He claimed to hate them. I thought back to the night he flipped out at Bria and me. My mind raced. Why was he there? So many possibilities flooded my mind. Was he there to spew his racist hatred even more? Did he want to break us up again? No, that couldn't be it. Bria had just saved Kimmy's life. Maybe he was there to say thank you. Yeah, that had to be it. But if that was all it was, why was he there alone? I had left my mom at the hospital with Kimmy. And come to think of it, I was pretty sure Bria's dad was still working at the hospital as well. If Patrick was thanking the Brownings, he was only thanking Bria's mom. I got a sick feeling in my stomach. A thought I didn't want to think slithered its way into my subconscious: my father was having an affair with Bria's mom.

I was overreacting. There was no way this was true. But if it were true, how long had it been going on? I stopped my mind from going where it wanted to go. I was being ridiculous. There was absolutely no way Patrick Vaughn was having an affair with Annette Browning. She was way too sophisticated for him. She shopped in Paris and threw galas at $1,500 a plate. Patrick Vaughn, unfortunately, was used to banging waitresses from Denny's while he was on the road. There was no possible way that they could have been having an affair for eighteen plus years.

Still, I decided to do a little investigating just to prove that an affair was not at all possible. I parked across the street and stared at the front door, waiting for him to exit. I didn't know what that would tell me. I thought I would be able to read their body language with each other and ... and ... and I didn't know what. Would I really be able to tell if they were cheating on their spouses simply from the way he walked out of the house? Probably not, but I was hoping there would be something obvious I could observe that would allay my fears. There had to be some logical explanation as to why he was there.

About ten minutes later, Patrick came storming out of the front door. He was almost to his car door when Annette stepped out onto her porch with her arms crossed. Patrick turned around and yelled, "You're a liar! Stay away from us."

Instead of responding, Annette Browning just shrugged then stepped back through the door. Then my father got into his car and sped off.

I had no idea what to make of the situation. Part of me wished that Bria was with me so she could come up with one of her theories. The other part of me was so happy she wasn't. She didn't need this on top of everything she was going through. I couldn't tell her about this in her condition. I had to keep this a secret, at least for a while.

I didn't realize how long I had sat in my car thinking about the situation. But before I knew it, Annette was leaving as well. I snapped out of my trance and pulled in the driveway. Using Bria's keys, I entered the house and headed upstairs to her room. I hadn't been in her room since before we broke up the first time a year ago.

We actually used to hang out in her room a lot. Since her parents weren't around much, her house was ideal for two teenagers. Fortunately for the Browning house, Bria and I were not typical teenagers. We didn't drink or throw wild parties. Our idea of a fun night was curling up together in front of the TV and watching classic ice skating performances on YouTube. Though Bria was not an ice skater by any means, she not only didn't mind watching skating performances but she loved to hear me explain the details of the jumps and the scoring and the difference between the long program and the short program. It didn't bore her like it did some of my other girlfriends. And she didn't just listen attentively because she loved seeing me be happy, but it was also because she just flat out loved to learn. She loved to learn about anything and that included the ins and outs of the skating world.

~~~

One night as we cuddled, she asked me about toe jumps versus edge jumps.

"You can tell by the takeoff," I said as I played a clip of Brian Boitano from the 1998 Olympics. "If they are bending the knee to launch, then it is an edge jump like a Salchow, a loop or an Axel. If they use the toe pick of their free leg, then it is a toe jump like a toe loop, flip or Lutz."

"Can you do all the jumps? Which is the most difficult?" she asked.

I nodded slowly. "Yeah, I can do all the jumps somewhat. And I don't really think about them in terms of difficulty because I mean what might be hard for one person could be easy for another. It's kind of like what you told me about the different types of math, right? Like some people who are good at geometry might hate algebra and vice versa."

Bria smiled. "Hey, you actually listen to me."

"I literally hang off your every word. I would listen to you talk for twenty-four hours a day if I could," I said, kissing her on the cheek as she giggled sweetly. "Anyway, so I don't think of them in terms of which is the hardest. I think of it in terms of what jumps give the most points."

"Well, which jump gives the most points?"

"The Axel is worth the most points. More specifically, the triple Axel."

"What makes it so hard?" Bria turned away from the TV and faced me. Her soft lips were inches away but I resisted the urge to feel them against mine again in order to impart my skating knowledge. It was the one thing in the world I knew more about than she did and it made me feel good to talk about it with her.

"Well, it looks completely different from the other jumps because you take the jump head-on. And because you start the jump from the front, the triple Axel is actually three and a half rotations."

"Can you do one?"

Instead of answering, I kind of grinned.

"You can, can't you?" she said.

"It's actually pretty exhilarating."

Bria sat up. "Why haven't you done a triple Axel in one of your routines?"

"It's not that simple, Bree."

"Why not?"

"I'm a pairs skater. I can't just randomly do a triple Axel in the middle of our routine."

Bria stared at me for a second. "Kimmy can't do one, can she?"

"It's not her fault. A triple Axel is so difficult that Mao Asada is the only woman that even attempts it regularly."

"So why don't you do it alone?"

"You mean be a solo skater? I can't abandon Kimmy. We started this together and we're gonna finish it together."

"Why can't you do both? Why can't you be a pairs skater and an individual skater?"

"I know they seem similar but pairs and individual are completely different worlds. It's not like tennis where you can have a solo career and just pick up a partner for a doubles match. The rules and scoring change between the divisions. I mean, for example, there is a scoring deduction for workload. If it appears one partner is doing more work than the other, then there is a penalty."

"So, in your routine, if you did a triple axel and Kimmy only did a double, you would be penalized?"

"Yep."

"That doesn't seem fair."

"Well, we have to be perfectly synchronized. Perfectly matched."

"You're still doing it," she said after staring at me for a few moments.

"Doing what?"

"Holding yourself back."

I sat up and reached for my soda. It was so gross I almost gagged. Bria had to know I was just trying to avoid this conversation since I never took more than one sip of a soda even though I asked for one each time I came over.

"I'm not holding myself back. I'm a pairs skater. I just am."

"Then how do you know you can do a triple Axel?"

"Because I tried it and I can do it."

"Just once?" she asked sitting up as well and facing me on the bed. "If it was just once, maybe you only landed it because of luck."

"It wasn't just luck, okay? I've landed over a hundred of them."

Bria did that thing with her lips she always does when she knows she's about to win a chess match. Did she think she was about to win this debate?

"Xanadu. Sweetie. Why would you practice a jump you can never do in a routine a hundred times?"

"Just to see if I can do it."

"That would justify one, maybe two successful jumps. But one hundred successful completions show either you're trying to prove something to yourself or you really enjoy doing triple Axels. Which is it?"

I took a long swig of soda to avoid having to respond.

"Either way, Xander, it shows that you should be doing triple Axels. And if you can only do it in an individual routine, then maybe you should be doing individual routines."

124

I couldn't argue with her logic. I actually couldn't think of anything to say to that. She sensed that I was uncomfortable so she added, "Can I see you do one?"

"Yeah, yeah, of course," I said happy to have a slight change of focus.

"Promise?"

"I promise," I said after a kiss.

Chapter 21: Bria

Xander's surprise was bringing me my schoolbooks, my computer, and my headphones. All of them. Most people thought it was simply for style reasons why I had a different color set of headphones for each day of the week, but Xander knew better. He knew how much it meant for me to have the right color headphones for the correct day of the week. He knew it would make me feel better. He also knew that having my schoolbooks and being able to get work done would relax me as well.

"My pens!" I yelled in excitement as I saw my twelve-pack of fine point roller gel pens. "You remembered!"

"Of course, I did," he said. "The orange one was missing so I stopped at Staples and bought you a new pack."

"I love you so much," I said, tears welling in my eyes.

"Bria Browning, you are seriously the best girlfriend a guy could ask for," he said, sitting next to me. "I mean, all I have to do is buy you a pack of pens or a puzzle and you declare your love for me." He leaned down and kissed me. He had to be the most amazing kisser on the planet. I didn't have much to compare it to, but I couldn't imagine anyone being better at it.

"You're the best boyfriend ever," I said. "I can't believe you remembered my special pens!" I exclaimed, holding the new pack of pens to my chest as if I was hugging a newborn baby.

"You are so weird," he said. "And I love every weird bone in your body." He kissed me again and then stood up as if to leave. But instead he just stared at me.

"What?" I asked.

He shrugged. "I just don't know what would make me think you would write that letter to me," he said. "I feel so stupid. If anything, you would have handwritten it using turquoise ink from your favorite pen collection."

I nodded. It was true. I had actually written notes to him while we were together the first time and they were always with the turquoise ink. That was my color for him. "Don't feel bad. I fell for the text message. We were both idiots."

We let the silence between us set as we thought about the breakup in our own way. I was sure he was running through the who and the why in his mind just as I had earlier. I had my theories about who, but since I didn't have a why, I decided to just keep it to myself.

"Well, I'm gonna go see Kimmy," he said finally. "You gonna be okay for a little while?"

"I've got my headphones, my pens, and an essay to write. I'm great."

"So weird," he said, shaking his head as he left my room.

After he left, I opened my computer intending to start my English essay, but instead that nagging doubt popped into my head and I found myself googling haploidentical match.

Chapter 22: Xander

I was still thinking about my breakup with Bria when I arrived at Kimmy's room a few minutes later. I should have been dwelling on the positive, that I had her back. But I couldn't stop thinking of the fact that someone had purposely split us up. Why would anyone do that?

"What are you thinking about?" Kimmy asked me when I got to her room. I told her about the text message and the letter that caused Bria and I not to speak for eleven months.

"I need to puke," she said. It was the chemotherapy. As I helped her to the toilet, I thought about the fact that my girlfriend's blood was flowing through my sister's body. Even though they didn't have the same blood type, because Bria had donated her bone marrow (the thing that creates the blood), slowly that bone marrow could possibly start creating the same blood type it was genetically programmed to.

My girlfriend had saved my sister's life.

"It was me," Kimmy said, wiping vomit from her mouth. I tied what was left of her hair back and then wiped her face with a cool cloth.

"What was you?" I asked as I flushed the toilet, ridding both of us of the sight of her latest deposit.

"I did it. It was my fault." Kimmy tried to lie down on the bathroom floor, but I wouldn't let her. I helped her to her feet. Once she was standing, I swept her up into my arms and carried her back to her bed.

"What was your fault, Kimmy?" I said once I had tucked her in snuggly. I grabbed the basin and placed it right next to her head in case she got the urge to vomit again.

"Your breakup with Bria."

"Kimmy, that wasn't your fault okay? We broke up because of the way Patrick treated her." After talking with Bria, I knew that wasn't completely true. But I also knew that Kimmy had nothing to do with the situation, or so I thought.

Kimmy was shaking her head violently. I thought she needed to puke again so I held up the basin, but she pushed it away. "You have to listen to me. I sent the text."

"What text?"

"The text message to Bria saying that you never wanted to see her again."

My heart sped up. Under normal conditions I would have yelled angrily at my little sister. My first instinct was to imitate Patrick in ways I didn't want to. I wanted to punch a wall or something but I resisted. She was so weak, so sick. How could I yell at her? I couldn't do that now. Not in the condition she was in, so I had to force myself to stay calm. "Why would you do that? Did Patrick make you do it?"

"She said I had to."

"She? Mom? Why?"

"She said that Bria was convincing you to go solo. She said that she was poisoning you against me. The only way I could keep our partnership together was to get rid of her. So when you went to sleep that night, I snuck into your room, sent the text, then deleted the conversation."

I couldn't respond.

"I'm so sorry, Xan. I didn't realize—"

"What? You didn't realize what?" I said, still trying to remain calm. It was taking all of my strength to keep from yelling. "That I was in love with her and that losing her ... " I couldn't even finish the sentence, thinking about all the pain I went through after our breakup. I didn't take it well at all and ended up picking up a pretty bad drinking habit and falling into some pretty serious self-destructive behavior.

"I'm so—"

"And then you sat there for nearly a year and watched me ache for her. You watched me stare at my phone night after night wondering why she didn't contact me. You saw me swipe through my collection of twelve pictures I had of her over and over again. You saw me sneak into chess tournaments just so I could get a glimpse of her. You saw me nearly drink myself to death and you said nothing?" This didn't feel right. It didn't feel right to be berating my baby sister while she was going through chemotherapy. I didn't know what to do. I wanted to yell and scream at her, but I couldn't. I felt cheated once again. I was cheated out of a year of happiness with Bria and now I was cheated out of my justified anger at the one who had prevented that happiness.

We sat in silence as I kept brushing the side of Kimmy's face. I couldn't hate her. I couldn't be mad at her. She was dying before my eyes. I wasn't allowed to hate her. And that made me even more angry.

I tried to focus on what was important. Kimmy's health. Once she was healthy, then I would yell at her. Maybe. In the long run, it really didn't matter. Sure, Kimmy was the one that aided and abetted our breakup, but she was also the one that convinced me to tell Bria how I felt and got us back together.

"Do you forgive me?" she asked.

"I ... I ... I don't know," I said honestly.

"That's fair," she said, stealing my catchphrase. "I don't really forgive myself actually. To think, what I did to you and her all because I thought she was some evil, brother-stealing villain and then she turns around and saves my life. I don't deserve her."

She was certainly right about that. No one could ever deserve Bria Browning. She was all that was right and pure and wonderful in life. She was brilliance and love personified and I was the luckiest person on the planet that she was able to love me in return. Just being near her made me a better person. I took a deep breath and forced myself not to blame Kimmy for missing a year of Bria. Instead I shifted that blame to my parents. They were the real reason we weren't together for all that time. Yes, they had manipulated Kimmy into breaking us up. But why?

Chapter 23: Xander

I wanted to be mad at Kimmy. I wanted to hate her even for a little bit. But how could I? She needed my love and support, not my anger. At the same time, I hated myself for even wanting to hate my sister. What a selfish thing to do. Why was I only thinking of myself?

This wasn't fair. None of this was supposed to happen. I wasn't supposed to lose Bria. My sister wasn't supposed to get cancer. My girlfriend wasn't supposed to almost die trying to save my sister's life. None of this was right. I needed to talk to someone. I needed help processing these emotions, but who could I talk to? My parents were out of the question. My normal go to sounding boards were Kimmy and Bria and both of them needed to focus on getting better, not trying to ease my emotional temper tantrum. The only thing I could do was skate through the pain.

It had been almost three weeks since I'd been to the rink. I went once right after Kimmy made me promise I'd go, but I hadn't been back since. I had rarely left her side. When I did leave her, it was to be with Bria. I hadn't even allowed myself to think about my skating career or my future. If I did, that would force me to think about Kimmy's future. Our careers were intertwined. We were a team. A partnership. Kimmy had our whole career planned out. She wanted us to make the Olympics within four years. Given her condition right now, that was just not going to happen. Even if she made a full recovery, this season was shot. Next season would be used to get her strength back. It would be at least three seasons before we were even competitive again. That was the best-case scenario. I didn't want to think about the worst-case scenario. Honestly, it wouldn't be too bad. I would a slight break from skating for a while like we talked about. I'd support Bria while she was at Stanford. Waiting a few years before our Olympic run wouldn't be the end of the world. There had been plenty of pair couples that continued to medal or even medaled for the first time well into their thirties. It could happen for us as well.

As I slowly skated through my warm-up, I allowed my mind to wander. I thought about the many people over the years who wondered why I wasn't an individual skater. I thought about that conversation with Bria in her bedroom about the triple Axel. Even she thought I could do it. Why didn't I? I started skating round and round the rink gathering speed, then, when it felt right, I leaped into a triple Axel. I landed it. I landed it well. And it felt good. I felt a rush. I needed to do it again. So, I did. And then again. Suddenly, I heard clapping from the stands.

"Who's there?" I asked the darkness. I thought I was alone. I had asked the manager for a favor and he'd let me in before the place had even opened.

Instead of answering, the person joined me on the ice. I couldn't believe my eyes. It was Marci Wong, two-time Olympic gold medalist.

"Oh my God! You're Marci Wong," I said as she skated circles around me.

"I am Marci Wong, but I am not God," she said with a chuckle. "And you are Alexander Vaughn. Eighteen-year-old rising skating star. And dare I say future gold medalist?"

"You know who I am?"

"Of course, I do," she said, doing a quick spin. "I always keep up with new talent. Honestly, I'm kind of surprised you know who I am. I medaled before you were born."

"My sister and I are huge fans. It's because of your costumes from the 90s that she makes me wear sequins in every competition."

Marci laughed again. "I am not sure whether to take that as a compliment or not."

"It's a compliment. Trust me."

"How is your sister, by the way?" she asked. "Aplastic anemia is serious."

"We found a donor and she had the transplant four days ago. So far, her body is reacting well to it."

"That's good. That's really good." Marci stopped skating circles around me and stood still as an awkward pause ensued. I could tell she wanted to ask me something but was holding back for some reason. "I would like to ask you something that might seem a bit ... indelicate," she began. "I wasn't planning on speaking with you about it at all for a while, given your current set of circumstances, but then Oscar let me into the rink early today to check it out and I saw you here practicing and I took it as a sign."

"A sign for what?" I asked.

She took a deep breath and said, "I want to be your choreographer."

"What? Serious? I didn't even know you did that?"

"I don't, but I want to. You would be my first."

"Wow! I mean, I'm honored. I'm totally honored. But with Kimmy's condition, I'm not sure when we'd be in need for a choreographer."

Marci Wong looked down and dug her toe pick into the ice. "Actually," she said after a moment, "I wasn't extending the invitation to your sister."

I was stunned speechless. I had no idea what to say. She wanted me as an individual skater? This was not how this usually worked. Usually the skater had to go in search of a coach or choreographer. It was a process that could take months. It could even take years before you found the perfect fit. To have someone ... No, not someone ... to have a former Olympic gold medalist ask to do your choreography was unheard of.

"I knew this was a mistake," she said when I didn't respond. "It's so completely insensitive of me. I don't know what I was thinking. Of course, you don't want to abandon your sister in her time of need. I just ... I just saw you out here skating and you landed three triple Axels in a row with ease. Not just ease, I mean you get like a foot higher than any other skater I have ever seen. And I would ask why you have never done the jump in competition, but I already know. In pairs, you can't do that jump if your partner can't so you've never had the opportunity to do the jump. But with the speed and height you're getting you could do a quadruple. You, Alexander, could be the first person in history to land a quadruple." She paused for a moment to gauge my response to her rambling rant that seemed to get faster and faster. I didn't know what to say to fill the void of silence. "Anyway," she continued, "it's not just your jumps. It's...it's you! You have this combination of explosive power mixed with grace that I have never seen before. You are a star, Alexander, plain and simple. I saw your potential and I wanted a piece of it. It was insensitive. I should not have asked."

This time when she stopped her rambling I said, "It's okay." And then there was another awkward silence that I wasn't sure how to fill.

"Well, I'm going to go crawl into a hole now," she said, heading to the exit.

"Um," I said before she stepped off the ice. She turned around and looked at me, waiting for me to finish my sentence. "You really think I can have a solo career?"

Marci nodded furiously with her eyes wide. "Surely, I am not the first person to tell you this."

"No, you're not."

Marci took her cell phone out of her pocket. "Do you have an iPhone?" she asked. "Do me a favor and watch this video I'm air dropping to you," she said after I nodded. "I recorded you for a good twenty minutes this morning. Let your coach watch it, let your parents watch it." She paused. "Okay, maybe not your parents. They have enough to think about right now. But just take a look at it and compare it to footage of the last three Olympic male figure skating medalists when they were eighteen. If you can explain to me how you are not better than them, then I will never broach the subject again."

Chapter 24: Xander

My mind was reeling from meeting Marci Wong. I should have been flat out thrilled that I not only met her but that she had heard of me and wanted to work with me. If I was being honest with myself, part of me immediately wanted to take her up on her offer just to get back at Kimmy for what she did to me. But the other part of me, the big brother part, realized that it would completely devastate her. I didn't know what to do. As I walked toward Kimmy's room, I knew it was not the time to bring up Marci Wong.

In fact, as soon as I entered the room, I should have just turned around and went back to the rink because ... my parents were there.

Both of them.

Somehow I had avoiding being with both of them at the same time for any extended period of time. They were much more tolerable individually. Together they were like gasoline and a match.

I entered Kimmy's hospital room quietly and took a seat as I observed my parents. My mother was standing over a sleeping Kimmy while Patrick was leaning against the bathroom door.

"Did the doctor say how long before she can get back to skating?" my mother asked my father.

"What the hell is wrong with you?" Patrick asked. "She's going through chemotherapy. And you're trying to pressure her into training?" I hated to admit it, but I agreed with Patrick on this one.

"I am not pressuring her to do anything," my mother said. "She loves to skate. It makes her happy. Maybe skating a little will help her get strong and feel better. Like skate therapy."

"Sure, that's what you thought. You really care about what's good for other people," he said sarcastically. "I've known you for twenty years and I've never seen you care about anyone but yourself."

"Don't start this nonsense now," she interrupted him.

"Why not, Nadia?"

"Because Kimmy is sick and she needs us to be positive."

"I am positive. I'm positive you're a psycho, selfish bitch."

"Patrick!" I yelled standing. "Not here. Not now." I thought my mother would pick up on my attempt to diffuse the situation. I was wrong. Instead she picked up the lamp on the nightstand, yanked it out of the wall and threw it at his head. The lamp missed him so she leapt into action and tried to attack him. He grabbed her arm midair as she tried to land a punch. He twisted her arm around her back and threw her to the ground.

By this point Kimmy had woken up. She joined me in staring in shock at our parents getting into a fistfight right in front of our eyes. To be honest, we weren't that shocked by the fighting itself. We had seen it before a number of times. We were just shocked that it was happening in a hospital room. And not just any hospital room. The room of their daughter who was possibly dying.

Nurse James heard the commotion and tried to separate them. Next, a security guard arrived and then the police. My dad was arrested for domestic disturbance even though it was my mother who had thrown the first lamp and punch. To top it all off, they were both banned from the hospital. Which meant, I would be the only family Kimmy would have while she was recovering.

Still in a haze of disbelief, I stayed with Kimmy to calm her down. When she fell asleep, I went to visit Bria. I really wanted to tell her about Marci Wong, especially since I couldn't tell my sister right now.

When I got to her room I found her packing. Well, trying to pack. She could barely walk so she was scooting around her room using the walker the hospital had given her.

"What are you doing?" I asked.

"Good news," she said. "I am getting out of here today."

"There is no way they are releasing you. There must be some mistake."

"Nope," she said. "They said I'm out of danger. I can't go back to school yet or anything but at least I'll be able to sleep in my own bed as I recover. I will have to start physical therapy to learn to walk properly again."

I wasn't sure how I felt about this. I mean, I was happy that she was well enough to go home, but I kind of liked having her in the hospital so near to Kimmy. Now it would be harder for me to split my time between the two of them. I felt so selfish for that thought. Which made me feel even worse for the topic I was about to bring up.

"You okay?" Bria asked.

"Yeah, yeah," I said. I took her hand and led her to the bed. "Please sit. I'll pack for you, okay?"

She nodded and sat down. I could tell she was already tired.

"What's going on?" she said when she caught her breath.

"It's nothing really. It's just that … Um, something happened this morning."

"The fight between your parents? Yeah, I heard."

"Yes, No. That's not what I'm talking about." Honestly, I was so used to my parents fighting I had kind of already forgotten about it. "No, I'm talking about something else. Something about me."

"Are you okay?" she asked with panic filling her eyes.

"Yes, I'm fine. Bria, relax."

She breathed a sigh of relief. "Dude, seriously, with our luck, I thought you were about to tell me you had Ebola or something."

I kissed her forehead. "No, I'm okay, Bria Bear. In fact, I'm better than okay. I went skating this morning."

Bria smiled. "Finally," she said. "I'm glad. I'm sure you needed that."

"There's more," I said. "I met Marci Wong."

"Olympic Gold medalist Marci Wong? Kimmy's idol Marci Wong? That Marci Wong?"

I nodded. "Well, what happened?" she asked.

I took her hand and sat next to her. "She wants to choreograph a routine for me."

Bria's mouth dropped open. I loved how she knew what a big deal this was for me. "She took video of me at practice this morning." I took out my phone and queued up the video and showed it to her. "Are you crying?" I asked a few seconds later.

"You're so beautiful, Xander," she said. "It makes me so happy to see you skating again."

I brushed her tears away with my thumbs. "You know you have to do this, right?" she said as I cradled her face in my hands.

I shook my head. "I can't. I can't skate without Kim."

"The video from this morning says otherwise."

"Well, I *can* skate without her but I don't *want* to. How do you think she is going to feel if I do? I don't even want to tell her that I met Marci Wong without her."

Bria kissed my hand. "You are so sweet, and loving and kind," she said. "Doing two or three competitions without your sister doesn't mean you don't love her."

"Doesn't it?"

"No, it doesn't. Why don't you talk to her about it? I'm sure she will agree with me. I'm sure she wants to see you skate as much as I do whether it is with her or without her."

"You think?"

"Well, let's think about this logically. It is going to take years before she's strong enough to skate competitively again. Why not use that time on developing your individual program? And then, when she's ready to return, you'll still be in shape and able to help her get back to form."

"Or, I could take a break from skating and go to college with you."

"Why would you want to do that?"

"Ouch," I said, feigning hurt but I was actually a little hurt that she wouldn't want me with her in school.

"And I'm not trying to say I don't want to be with you. I would run away with you today and live in a cave for the rest of my life if it meant being with you forever."

My heart melted. That was the most sentimental thing she had ever said to me. Bria was not great with expressing her emotions. So every time she even told me she loved me it was an unexpected thrill. For her to use such a hyperbole to express her feelings was beyond thrilling.

I smiled and then kissed her. "I love you, too."

"What I am trying to say," she said, putting her hand on my chest and pushing me away. I noticed, she didn't return my kiss with as much energy as I would have thought. "What I tried to tell you a year ago is that you should seriously consider a solo career. And I know you think it's a bad time because Kimmy is sick, but honestly, this may actually be the best time. She can't skate with you right now and it could be years until she can again. Why not take that time to prepare for one competition and see how it goes?"

I was less concerned with what she was saying than how she reacted to my kiss.

"Are you okay, Bria?"

"Yeah, I'm fine," she said, turning away from me. "Do you want to give me a ride home?"

"Sure."

Chapter 25: Bria

I was conflicted. I knew there had to be a reason why I was a haploidentical match for Kimmy's bone marrow transplant. According to the internet, that reason was that I was Kimmy's half-sister, but I didn't want to believe that reason. Part of me was inclined to ignore it and let myself be in love with Xander and let him kiss me as much as he wanted. But then my brain got to work and I realized that I have to be related to the Vaughns. My stupid brain. Why couldn't I ignore it? I was sure I had completely confused Xander, but I didn't know what else to do. I couldn't tell him anything until I was sure.

"Will you let me carry you up the stairs?" Xander asked after he had helped me inside the house.

"That's not really necessary, Xan," I said.

"Come on, Bree. Let me help you. Plus, you would be helping me as well."

I gave him a 'yeah, right' look. "And how exactly would I be helping you?"

"I haven't had a workout in weeks. I'm getting flabby. I need to build up my strength again if I'm going to go into training for a solo routine."

I smiled at him. "You've decided to call Marci Wong?"

He nodded and at the same time swept me up into his arms and headed up the stairs. I let him. What was I supposed to do? Leap out of his arms? I could barely walk.

I actually needed the help. Walking up those stairs would have taken me twenty minutes. Besides he smelled so good. I buried my face in his chest and just inhaled. He had been practically living in the hospital for the past two weeks. How had he managed to still smell like this?

Xander set me down gently on my bed and lingered momentarily. I could hear his heart beat and his breath quicken. This could have been the moment when it happened. We were completely alone. We were in love. And we were on my bed. Sex was the natural next step, right?

We'd had the conversation before. Back when we were together the first time, I was the one to bring it up much to his surprise.

~~~

"Are you a virgin?" I asked him frankly while we were drinking cocoa in his basement. We had been together for a little over four months at that point and things were going extremely well. We'd had several seriously passionate make-out sessions, but it never progressed any further. I didn't think it was because either of us didn't want to. I just thought it was because neither of us knew where the other stood on the subject so I thought it was time to talk about it.

Xander nearly choked on his drink. After a short coughing fit he said, "Um, why?"

"Oh, was that inappropriate to ask? I was just curious. I thought as your girlfriend I was allowed to know."

"No, yes. I mean … " Xander set down his mug and took a deep breath. "No, it's not inappropriate to ask. And yes as my girlfriend you should know my ... sexual history."

"Why did you say it like that?"

"Like what?"

144

"Like you're embarrassed by the word sex. It's nothing to be embarrassed about. It's a very natural biological act that happens to be rather pleasurable."

Xander's eyes expanded. "So … you've had sex before?" he asked.

"God no," I said. "Don't be ridiculous."

"Why is that a ridiculous question? You just said that sex was natural and pleasurable. Why is it then ridiculous for me to assume that you have done it?"

"Okay, I can see how that would be misleading," I said.

Xander took a sip of cocoa then said, "I'm a virgin as well."

For some reason that made me feel good. Oh, who was I kidding? I knew exactly why it made me feel good. I wanted him to be my first and I wanted to be his.

"I have done a lot of research on the subject," I said.

"Of course, you have," Xander said with a smile. "I would expect nothing less from you."

"Well, after extensive research, I have come to the conclusion that in deciding to have sex for the first time, the three main factors are the who, the where, and the when. I've decided the where should be my bedroom. My bed is extremely comfortable and cozy and worthy of such an event. There is no way I am having sex in the back seat of a car or in some locker room or something. That would be uncomfortable and downright unsanitary. I want my first time to be in my room."

"How do you know my bed isn't just as comfortable?" He was teasing me with that question but I didn't mind. I knew it wasn't mean-spirited like some of the people in school when they asked me questions. When Xander teased me, his eyes smiled. His turquoise blue eyes lit up with joy and it made me feel like I put that joy there.

"Yes, your bed is comfy but your room smells like sweaty socks."

"That's fair," he said with a nod. "Continue."

"So, the where is easy: my bedroom. The who is easy as well. It's you."

Xander choked on his cocoa again. "Me? You're sure?"

"Of course, I'm sure. I wouldn't say it if I wasn't."

"How do you know you want me to be your first?"

I sighed. I wish I had some sort of formula or equation or something to provide an evidentiary basis for my decision, but no such thing existed. "I just know you'll never hurt me."

Xander placed his fingers in my hair and brought my face toward his. "I will never, ever hurt you, sweet Bria," he whispered before kissing me. "What about the when?" he asked, our lips still practically touching.

"November 2nd."

"Wait, what?" he said, pulling away from me slightly.

"I want to have sex with you on November 2nd."

"What? Why?" Xander sat up and scooted away from me on the couch as if my peculiarities had finally terrified him. "I'm confused. Why that date? It's not your birthday or mine. It's not a holiday or anything. What's so special about November 2nd?"

"That's the date I'm going to have sex for the first time. With you." I was confused as to why he was confused. Didn't I just go through this?

Xander held in a grin as he asked, "But why that specific date, Bria? Why November 2nd and why not any other day of the year like ... today, for example?"

"You want to have sex with me today?" I asked.

"I mean, I don't NOT want to. I mean, I'm ready any time you are. I just want to know why you chose November 2nd."

I turned away from him. I was embarrassed. If I told him the real reason, he would think I was completely insane and I would lose him. But he'd asked and I hated lying. Plus, if I told him the truth and he didn't think I was insane, that would make me love him even more. Yeah, I knew after just a few weeks of dating him that I was completely in love with him. Well, if I were being honest, I knew I loved him after a few hours of talking to him during that first newspaper interview. I hadn't told him yet. I didn't want to tell him as it was too soon and I didn't want to scare him away.

"Bria," he said, rubbing my back. "Why November 2nd?" he asked again. I sighed. I had to tell him.

I turned to him and said, "I have a very weird brain."

He shrugged and said, "I like that about you. I like the way you think."

Not for long, I thought to myself. "I have this thing called synesthesia. It's where your senses cross. Like some people can see sounds or taste colors."

Xander looked extremely confused. His mouth opened but no words formed.

"For me, it's different. I see numbers as colors, days of the week have feelings and months have a smell. And for me, November 2nd is the exact color of your eyes and it feels like a hug from ... you."

Xander kept staring at me without saying anything. That was it, I thought. I had completely lost him. He was going to think I was some kind of lunatic.

Finally, he said, "That is the coolest thing I have ever heard in my life."

"Really?"

"Um, yeah. You're like a superhero. My girlfriend has super powers!" He stood up then picked me up and tossed me over his shoulder while tickling my belly. "Do something super power-y!" he yelled. "Quick, what color is 3,281?"

"It's a precise swirl mixture of red, turquoise blue, white and green," I said while laughing.

Xander spun me around the basement as we both laughed and giggled.

"Okay, okay, What about seventy-two? What does it look like? How does it feel?"

"Seventy-two is a bright, sunny yellow with a white tail. And it feels like floating on yellow Jell-O." I said, laughing at how ridiculous it sounded out loud. It was so crazy that I had never told anyone about it. Except for that first time when I described it to my mom when I was about five and she looked at me like I was an alien. I never told anyone else about it after that. It was so freeing to be able to say it out loud and not have him think something was wrong with me.

"That is incredible," he said, still spinning me. He flipped me off of his shoulder and into a cradle hold. "Is that why you wear a different color pair of headphones every day?"

I nodded. "Music just sounds better if you wear the color that matches the day."

Xander laughed so hard I shook in his arms. "That is so crazy it's cute. Tell me something else," he said.

"Um, I have your driver's license number memorized. Not because I want to steal your identity or anything. It's just a really pretty color."

"Bria, I don't even know my own driver's license number."

Xander threw me up in the air and caught me. I felt like I was in one of his routines. Finally, he dropped me on the couch and leaned over me. "You amaze me, Bria Browning."

Tears welled in my eyes. Not only did I not scare him off, but he seemed to like me even more. How did I get so lucky? How did I manage to find someone that totally got me? Someone who let me be me and didn't judge me? In that moment, I really wished it was November 2nd already.

~~~

The memory of that conversation flashed in my head as Xander leaned over me on my bed. November 2nd had come and gone while we were not together. And now we were together but I suspected that we were related. Did we miss our chance?

Apparently, the November 2nd conversation had popped into Xander's head as well. I could tell by the way he looked into my eyes.

He needed to leave. Now.

"I'm in so much pain, Xander. I need to rest," I said, getting under my blanket and turning my back to him.

"Of course," he said as he tucked my hair behind my ear then kissed the side of my head. "Call me when you wake up," he whispered.

As soon as he left, I took out my computer and continued my research.

Chapter 26: Xander

My sister was a skeleton. Her vitals were good and it seemed like the transplant was working but she had no energy and kept losing weight. Her doctors were keeping her in the hospital until she stabilized more.

The sight of her was soul crushing. I tried to be upbeat and positive when I was with her, but it depleted me emotionally. On top of that, Bria was avoiding me. Every time I called her, she said she was tired and needed to rest. I hadn't even seen her since I dropped her off at home when she was released from the hospital. That was five days ago.

My only way to deal was to call Marci Wong. She was so thrilled that I had reached out to her that we met the very same day and had met every day after. We went to a different rink so as not to upset Renitsky. He was great and all as a coach and had done a lot for Kimmy and me, but I decided to think of him as my pairs coach and to think of Marci as my individual coach.

"How's Kimmy?" Marci asked while looking at a recording she had just taken of me.

I sighed. "The doctors say she's getting better but I don't see it."

Marci nodded, still not looking at me. "And what about your girlfriend?"

I looked a question at her. "I never told you I had a girlfriend."

"Didn't you?" she asked. "Well, if this Bria person isn't your girlfriend she needs to get a restraining order against you."

I felt my face flush. "Do I talk about her a lot?"

Marci nodded while still scrolling through her iPad. "Uh, yeah."

"Sorry."

"Look, you're a teenager in love," she said, looking at me for the first time. "I get it. It's normal. Most coaches will tell you no distractions. No girlfriends. No life. Whatever. I'm not like that."

"You're not?"

"Life happens. The world doesn't just stop because you're an amazing skater. Your sister gets sick or your girlfriend starts ghosting you, you have to skate through it."

"Wait. You think she's ghosting me? Why would she do that?"

"Look at this," Marci said as she held her iPad in front of my face. I started watching the footage of me on the ice. "It's incredible," she said. "It's absolutely fantastic until ... until ... right ... there. Did you see that?"

"Yeah, I couldn't land it."

"That's not what I saw," Marci said. "That's not what I saw at all. You could have absolutely landed it. But you touched the phone in your pocket. Were you trying to check and see if it was vibrating as if you wouldn't feel it against your butt?"

"So, I have too much on my mind to skate?" I asked.

"Nope. You have to use it. You may not ever have a time in your life when your mind can be completely free. So use it. Train yourself to use those worries as fuel."

"How do I do that?"

Marci sighed. "When I won my second gold medal, it was a very difficult time. My mother had just been diagnosed with Alzheimer's and I had just had a miscarriage."

"I didn't know that. How did you do that?"

"I didn't ignore it like some people will tell you and I didn't drown in the pain. I used the pain. I let it push me. Every jump I landed, every successful combination, I dedicated it to my baby and my mother."

"Don't try to ignore my problems, but embrace them?"

"Yes, let them motivate you to be better at whatever you do. Make it a game if you have to."

"What do you mean?"

"Give me your phone," she said. Normally, I wouldn't be skating with a phone in my pocket, but I didn't want to be too far away from it in case Kimmy or Bria called. I took it out of my pocket and handed it to her. "Now, give me ten perfect combinations in a row and I'll let you check to see if Bria called."

"Wait, what?"

"Go."

~~~

"Damn," Marci said twenty minutes later as she handed me my phone. "That was the best you have done all week."

"Did she call?" I asked.

Marci shook her head. "Nothing from Kimmy or Bria. But I get the feeling you were asking about Bria."

I didn't respond but I figured she knew the answer. "What is so special about this girl anyway?" Marci asked, leading me off the ice.

I put on my blade covers and sat on the bleachers closest to the entrance.

"You wouldn't understand."

Marci scoffed. "You think I've never been eighteen? Don't be an idiot. Tell me about her."

I took a deep breath and said, "I don't think the right adjectives have been invented to describe the level of amazing she is."

"Wow, high praise indeed coming from you. I mean, you're pretty amazing yourself. Does she skate as well?"

"Oh no, she can barely stand upright on ice unless I'm holding her hand. But she's good at everything else. And I do mean everything. She's a genius and the way she sees the world is just so unique and I like when I see myself through her eyes. And she has this thing called synesthesia where she sees numbers as colors. Isn't that the coolest thing you've ever heard?"

Marci smiled as I was talking. It was like my happiness was contagious. "And why isn't she talking to you anymore?"

"I have no idea. She donated the marrow that saved my sister's life. And she caught an infection from the donation and had to stay in the hospital for much longer than expected. And then I drove her home when she was released and she hasn't seen me since. Maybe she blames Kimmy or me for the infection. She has difficulty walking now. Oh no, what if she's permanently disabled?"

"Wait a minute. Your girlfriend donated the marrow that saved your sister's life?"

"Yeah, that's just the kind of girl she is. So selfless and loving."

"But, your girlfriend was a match to your sister?"

"Yeah, so?"

"That is quite a coincidence, don't you think?"

"No, it's not that much of a coincidence, is it? I mean, there's a registry for a reason, right? People find bone marrow transplant matches all the time."

153

Marci looked at her wrist as if she were wearing a watch. She wasn't. "Let's call it a day, shall we? You should probably get to school."

There was really no reason for me to get to school. My grades were shot. There was no way I was going to finish the semester on time. But the school was being really flexible with me and allowing me to complete my work on my own time. I was actually considering dropping out completely and finishing up with homeschool or just getting my GED. In any case, I saw no reason to go to school. I also didn't think it would be a good idea to show up at Bria's house. So instead, after a quick shower, I headed to the hospital to visit Kimmy.

Chapter 27: Xander

To my surprise, Kimmy was awake and sitting up when I went to her room. Her back was toward the door as she stared out the window. When she turned to me, I saw tears slowly streaming down her face.

"Kimmy, what's wrong? Are you in pain?"

She shook her head and wiped the tears away with the back of her hand. "Why aren't you going to school today?"

I shrugged. "I thought my time would be better spent with you."

"Xan, you can't keep skipping school. You're supposed to graduate this year. I can't have you flunk out. That would just be one more thing that's all my fault."

"What are you talking about?"

"Never mind," she said, crawling under the covers of her hospital bed.

"Do you need to talk to me about something?" I asked.

"I'm sorry, Xan," she said, fresh tears streaming down her cheeks again. She looked so small and weak in her bed. Her hair was completely gone and her eyes were sunk into reddish brown circles. Every time I looked at her for the past few days it felt like the wind was being knocked out of me. I couldn't believe that two months ago, this little girl was doing backflips on the ice. Now she looked as if she were about to shatter like a piece of ice.

"Sorry for what?" I said with a smile, trying to feign an upbeat attitude.

"I feel like I ruined your life."

"That's crazy. Why would you say that?"

"I know you don't love figure skating as much as I do. You do it for me."

"That's not true."

"Don't lie to me. I'm sick, not stupid."

"I'm not lying, Kim. I do love skating. You might be right about the competing part. I don't love competing. But I do love skating and I love you and I love making you happy."

"You're so good at it, Xan. You have no idea. You are the best. You could go to the Olympics. You can win in singles or with another partner. Just not Courtney Ballinger. I hate that girl. She always looks like she just smelled a fart."

I laughed. "Kimmy, I will never skate with anyone else but you for as long as I live."

"Don't say things like that. Please keep skating after I'm gone."

A lump formed in my throat and I had to force myself not to cry. "Kimmy—"

"I ruined Bria for you too," she said, interrupting me.

"What? You might have broken us up but you also got us back together."

She shook her head. "And now come to find out I'm the reason you can never be together."

"What are you talking about?"

"If I hadn't gotten sick, you would have never known and you could have lived happily ever after with her."

"Known what?"

"Xan, didn't you listen to anything she said about the donor registry and genetics and the probability of finding a match?"

I racked my brain trying to figure out what she was hinting at but nothing came to mind.

"Bria is a haploidentical match to me. She's black and I'm white. The only way that is even remotely possible is if she's our half-sister."

I don't actually remember what I said after that. I know I had to pretend not to be upset. I had to be strong so as not to make Kim feel worse. She needed the best possible environment if she was to recover.

Kim continued to rattle on about Nationals and the Olympics and purple sequined costumes while I smiled and nodded, pretending I wasn't flipping out inside.

Finally, she talked herself to sleep and I was able to slip out of her room. I had to see Bria and figure out what the hell was going on.

Chapter 28: Bria

I was walking better. I could make it to the bathroom and back to my bed without my walker, but that was about it. I still wasn't ready to go back to school. I wouldn't be able to stand the looks of pity from the aliens. I had crutches as well but those were so much trickier to use for me. A wheelchair honestly would have been the best, but I refused to go to school with a wheelchair. I would just have to learn to get by on crutches.

The school would probably assign someone to hold my books and help me around. Or worse yet, Xander would volunteer to do it. I couldn't bear to see him. Not until I was sure. Unfortunately, when I heard my front door open one morning, I knew it had to be Xander. He had helped me choose the hiding place for the extra key.

"You knew, didn't you?" Xander asked when I opened the door to my bedroom.

Xander had figured it out. I could hear the pain in his voice and it pained me. I had hoped for more time. I had hoped for definitive answers before I had to have this conversation. But it wasn't to be.

"I don't know how to answer that," I said honestly. I stepped aside and let him enter the room fully. I reached for the cane that my dad had brought home and used it to hold myself up.

Xander started pacing around my bed. "Just tell me the truth. This is the reason you've been ghosting me, isn't it? You know we have to be related."

"No, Xander, that's not the truth." I reached out to touch him and had to restrain myself. "The truth is, I need more information. The truth is, I don't know anything for sure."

"But you have a theory?" he asked as he finally stopped pacing and looked at me.

I nodded. "Three, actually."

"Tell me," he said.

I stared at him for a second. He looked so pale and hurt and broken. "Have you eaten?" I asked. "My parents got takeout. It's in the fridge. Why don't you make yourself a plate and we can talk while you eat?"

"I don't want to eat, Bria. I just want to know if you're my sis ... "

He choked on the word sister as if it was couldn't to make him wretch.

"Fine, sit down," I said, using my cane to point to the bed. Probably not a good idea to have him sit on my bed, but it was the best place to see my dry erase board where I had drawn up my theories so I could give him a quick tutorial on genetics.

"Kim and I have to be half siblings," I began after he took a seat on my bed. "We could even be whole siblings, technically, but given that I look black and she looks white that is rather unlikely. Possible, but not likely."

"So are you both mixed? How is this even possible?"

"It's confusing. But let's say all three of us are half white and half black. Even though you and Kim have blue eyes, it's still possible you are half black. The phenotype for blue eyes is recessive."

"What does that mean?"

I found an empty spot on my dry erase board and drew a chi-square table. "Even if two parents have brown eyes like your dad and my mom, they could still carry the recessive gene for blue eyes, meaning their children would have a one in four chance of having blue eyes. If just one parent has blue eyes and the other brown eyed parent carries the blue recessive gene, that increases to two out of four."

"I could be half black?" he asked.

"It's statistically possible." This wasn't helping. I wanted to stop talking. I didn't want to tell him anything else that would upset him, but he was determined to know. I took a deep breath and continued. "Now, since you and I have similar birth days—Unless, of course, they lied about our birth dates and we're actually twins which I find highly unlikely … "

I saw Xander physically shudder at the thought. I had to admit that that was particularly gross to think about.

"Let's take that off the table and agree that it is not possible that we have the same mother. Which leads me to the cheater theory. Either your mom cheated with my dad or my mom cheated with your dad."

Xander closed his eyes as he processed this information. I knew it had to be a gut punch since the cheater theory was highly likely. Patrick Vaughn, professional hockey player, was notorious for his extramarital affairs. Honestly, I didn't think my mother was his type, but that didn't mean it was out of the realm of possibility. I mean, maybe that was the reason he flipped out over Xander and I dating. Maybe it wasn't about race at all, but the fact that he knew Xander and I were half brother and sister.

Xander stood up and clutched the sides of his head so hard that I thought he was going to draw blood.

"So," I said in a calming voice, "I have outlined my theories on the board here with a couple of family trees. Here we have your dad and our moms and over here we have my dad and our moms," I said, pointing to the board.

"Same dad, different moms. Same dad, different moms." He kept repeating this while walking around my room. Suddenly, he stopped. "There's another possibility," he said, taking the marker out of my hand. He wiped off my chi squared chart and wrote Patrick, Nadia, Jeffrey and Annette in a line. Then under Patrick and Nadia, he wrote Xander. Under Nadia and Jeffrey, he wrote Kimmy and under Jeffrey and Annette, he wrote Bria. "There," he said. "What if you and Kimmy have the same father, but you and I share no blood at all? Did you think of that?"

I nodded as I choked back tears. "I did."

"Well, why didn't you add that to the list?" he asked.

I couldn't hold back the tears any longer. "Don't cry, Bree," he said as I collapsed in his arms. "I got you. I got you."

I pushed him away and tried to get control over my emotions. "Of course, I thought of it. Of course, that's what I want to be true. But I didn't mention it because I didn't want to get your—to get our hopes up, okay? I mean, in the unlikely event that we are not related by blood, that still means that your half sister is my half sister. Could you really live with that? Could you really be in love with your sister's sister?"

"I don't know. Maybe?" he said. "All I know is that I can't lose you. Not again."

I didn't want to, but I let him hug me.

"Can I kiss you?" he asked.

"We shouldn't."

"Please," he said breathlessly

"No, seriously, we shouldn't. Not until I do this." I limped over to my desk and grabbed the cotton swab I had set aside for this purpose. "Open up," I said before brushing it on the inside of his cheek.

"What was that for?"

"Paternity test," I said as I carefully placed the swab in the tube.

When I was done, he kissed me and I didn't stop him. My brain told me I should stop him. I should prepare myself for what was possible. But my heart told me just to believe the unlikely.

"You really think we should do a paternity test?" he asked after our stolen kiss. Something told me that might be our last one.

I shrugged. "We can either do a paternity test or talk to our parents," I suggested. "Whichever would be less painful."

"Paternity test it is," Xander said.

Chapter 29: Bria

I'm really smart. I'm not going to lie. But I am not as smart as people think I am. I'm pretty good at math and at memorizing facts. But I'm no genius or anything. I was sure Xander probably thought I was going to analyze our DNA samples right there in my bedroom. But I barely understood the process and I didn't have the right equipment. But I knew who did.

"Bria, what happened?" Gaganjyot Prabhakar asked as he saw me enter his lab on crutches.

"Long story."

"Say no more," he said as he gave me a big hug, his slightly overweight frame nearly suffocating me. "It's good to see you."

"You too, Gaganjyot," I said, even though I was barely able to breathe.

"Ah and there it is," he said.

"What?" I pushed him away and took a deep breath.

"The sound of someone properly pronouncing my name. I swear you say it better than my own mother." I smiled, thinking about the hours I spent over several days during my freshman year practicing the pronunciation. I found it completely unacceptable that people at school just started calling him Ali because they wouldn't take the time to learn it.

"Thank you for the compliment," I said in perfect Punjabi.

Gaganjyot's eyes widened in surprise. "Marry me, Bria Browning."

"Very funny," I said—in English, of course. That was about the extent of my Punjabi unless he wanted to talk about the weather or where I could find the bathroom. "How are you?" I asked.

"Much better now that you're here." He smiled and raised his eyebrows twice as if trying to hint at something.

It took all of my strength not to roll my eyes. I had to play nice. He was doing me a huge favor by running a paternity test for me in his lab. Sure, I was completely exploiting the fact that Gaganjyot had had a huge crush on me for the past three years, but I was desperate. I didn't want to have to send away my DNA to one of those online companies and wait weeks for a result. I needed an answer as soon as possible.

Gaganjyot was a biology major at the University of Colorado in Boulder so I knew he had access to a lab. I also knew that he knew enough about genetics to perform the test himself and give me a reliable answer quickly.

After the way I treated him a year and a half ago, he really should have just hung up the phone on me when I'd called and asked to meet him, but the way he was eager to help made me feel as though he thought he still had a chance.

Back when Gaganjyot was a senior and I was a junior, he made it clear he was interested in me.

Apparently, he'd had a crush on me since I was a freshman when I learned to say his name properly. I'd had no idea at the time. Anyway, he was the captain of the chess club and he made sure that we played each other at every practice. To be honest, I was flattered by the attention. No other boy had ever even looked twice at me.

I was just the little black girl that was completely invisible until someone needed help with their homework. I was okay with that too since I had never really been interested in anyone else. I had gotten used to being alone. That was until the newspaper assigned me to do an article on Xander Vaughn. Just the sight of him lit a fire in me. And talking to him only served to fan those flames.

I was a realist, so I realized that I had absolutely no chance at a relationship or anything with someone like Xander, but boy did I love having to interview him ... for three hours. And then, to my surprise, after that first interview, Xander called me up out of the blue to hang out. And then he did it again and again. I thought he was just making sure that I wrote a favorable article about him, but even after the article was published, he still wanted to hang out.

At the same time, Gaganjyot was asking to take me to the movies over and over again. Even though I really liked Xander, I knew there was no way he would want to be with me. He was beautiful and talented and on his way to being internationally famous. Why would he want a borderline math freak like me? Anyway, I eventually relented and agreed to go on a date with Gaganjyot. But the night of our scheduled date, Xander showed up at the school newspaper office and something amazing happened.

"Can we talk?" he had asked. I gave a confused look to Sarah, the only other person left in the office. She was confused as well but she politely left the room so Xander and I could be alone.

"Sure, what's on your mind?" I asked, trying to seem cool and relaxed when on the inside I was totally freaking out. I had no idea what he wanted to talk about, but I knew it had to have something to do with something wrong I had said or did. He was finally going to tell me he didn't want to be friends anymore or hang out with me. That had to be it.

Instead of answering, Xander took a deep breath and let it out slowly. "I can't do this here. I'm out of my element. Will you come with me?"

"Actually, I have—"

"Please." His eyes were wide and so blue and had this cute, begging puppy dog quality. It made me weak.

I glanced at my phone. I still had two hours before I was supposed to meet Gaganjyot so I said, "Sure."

Xander took me to the lake that was behind his house. He had bought me a pair of ice skates that somehow fit me perfectly.

"When was the last time you've been on the ice?" he asked.

"Probably when we were four," I reminded him, referring to his fourth birthday party and the picture of us hand in hand on skates.

"Don't worry, I got you," he said, taking both my hands and leading me onto the ice. He skated backwards effortlessly while I held on to him for dear life as he led me around the lake. After a few laps, I started to feel a bit more comfortable. Instead of holding both my hands and leading me around, he held one hand and skated next to me.

"We've been hanging out a lot for the past three weeks," he began as if he was reciting a prepared speech.

"Yeah," I said, not sure where he was going with this train of thought.

"It's been fun, right?" he asked.

"Yeah, totally." OMG. I sounded like such a nerd, but I couldn't think of anything else to say.

"So I was wondering if you, by any chance, would want to do that even more often?"

"What do you mean? I mean, we're already together a lot. Not that I have anything else to do or anything."

"I'm trying to ... Okay, this is weird ... "

"Oh, do you need help on your homework or something? Sure, I can tutor you. No problem." That had to be it. He needed a tutor and he was ashamed.

"No, no, Bria. That's not what I ... I mean, I probably do need one ... but that's ... " He stopped, took a deep breath and said, "Okay, I just want to know if you would like to be my girlfriend?"

"Me? You want me to be your girlfriend?"

"Uh, yeah," he said, obviously not expecting my reaction.

"Why?"

"Because I really like spending time with you and when you're not around all I do is think about you and wonder when will be the next time I will be able to see you. And I figure if we are boyfriend and girlfriend, I won't have to make up reasons for us to hang together. I can just say things like 'I want to see my girlfriend' or 'my girlfriend and I have plans' or 'I'm going out with my girlfriend.'"

At this point, my stomach was doing backflips. He wanted me, Bria Browning, to be his girlfriend. I didn't even know how to process that information. And because of that I was unable to respond.

Unfortunately, my lack of response made Xander think I was rejecting him.

"I'm sorry," he said after a few moments of silence. "I thought that you might like me as much as I like you. My mistake. No worries, we can still be friends. That is if you want to. If not, that's okay, too, I guess."

Unable to formulate actual words, I resorted to doing the thing I had wanted to do since the first moment I saw him three weeks ago. I kissed him.

"Wait, so, I'm confused," he said after my awkward yet still thrilling peck on his lips. His lips were so firm and kissable that I had been dreaming of them nonstop for weeks. They felt even better than I had imagined.

"Yes, I will be your girlfriend." *I can't think of anything in the world I want more.* Fortunately, I didn't say that part. Just thought it. Didn't want to come off as too desperate. Anyway, we spent the rest of the evening making out in his basement, which meant I totally forgot about my date with Gaganjyot.

"Oh my God! I'm late!" I shrieked suddenly two hours later. Xander had just gone upstairs to get us some hot cocoa. I started putting on my snow boots and looking for my scarf and gloves just as he returned.

"What happened? Where are you going?" he asked.

"I'm late. I forgot I have someplace to be."

"Late for what?" he asked. "Can't you just send a text and reschedule or something?"

"Text, yes. Genius. I'll just say I'm on my way. Can you take me back to my car please?"

Xander set down the cocoa and said, "I'll just take you wherever you need to go," as he put on his coat.

"No, that's okay. I can't really have my boyfriend drop me off on a date with another guy."

"Wait. What?" he asked.

"Oh, sorry. I'm so sorry." Now I was sure he was gonna dump me.

"God, Bria. We've been together for like two hours and you are already cheating on me."

My heart sank. I just knew it was over.

"I'm kidding. I'm totally kidding." Xander grabbed my scarf and pulled me close to him. "You weren't expecting this," he said, kissing me. "It's not your fault." I breathed a sigh of relief. "But why can't you just cancel by text? I mean, you're not really going to go through with the date, are you?"

"Of course not. But I'm also not going to dump him via text. I can't think of anything more cruel. I just need to talk to him face-to-face."

Gaganjyot was waiting outside the movie theater for me when I arrived. "Finally!" he said. "We're gonna miss all the previews. I love the previews."

"Gaganjyot, we have to talk," I said.

He wasn't as upset as I thought he would be that I was breaking our date. He just sighed and said, "Well, I hope he deserves you."

I looked at him skeptically. I hadn't said anything about Xander. Or about there being another person at all.

"Who?" I asked, curious as to how he figured it out.

He shrugged. "Not sure, but it's got to be someone. My guess would be the Vaughn kid, the ice skater. You have been talking about him incessantly for weeks now."

"Really?"

He nodded and then swept me up into one of his suffocating bear hugs. "Hope it works out for you."

~~~

And now here I was, a year and a half later, asking him to do a DNA test that would show whether the guy I dumped him for was actually my brother. It was too weird. Fortunately, I had the good sense not to tell him who the second sample belonged to.

"What am I doing with these?" he asked as he took the samples from me. "Do you need me to see if one is the father of the other?"

"No, I just need to know if the two samples have a parent in common."

"Okay, well that is not really a paternity test. This is a sibling test or more specifically a half sibling vs. unrelated."

"Is that a problem?" I asked.

"Depends on the degree of certainty you want. With a half sibling test, I can't really give you that Maury Povich moment where you know with 99 percent probability that the guy is the father. In fact, I may not be able to give you a conclusive result at all because the pattern of inheritance and degree of sharing of genetic markers between siblings are not the same as that between a parent and a child."

I slumped down in a chair. This was not what I wanted to hear.

"One of these is yours, isn't it?" I nodded. "So you might have a sibling." I nodded again. "I take it, that's not a good thing."

"I don't really want to talk about it."

"Okay, that's fine. Don't worry about it. Just know that I'm still a student so anything I find won't hold up in court."

I nodded. "That's fine. I just need to know."

Chapter 30: Xander

Bria went to take our DNA to her friend whose name I couldn't remember but who everyone called Ali. I didn't know how long it would take. Was it one of those things where it would take days or weeks like on Law & Order? Would he be able to put a rush on it? Or would it go faster because it was his lab? I had no idea. But instead of sitting around and dwelling on it, I decided to call up Marci for an impromptu rehearsal.

"I talked to Renitsky," she said before we got started.

"What? I thought you didn't want to tell him about us working together." I was so shocked by this development that I almost tripped walking to the ice.

"Yeah, that's what I thought initially, but then I realized that it is technically illegal to poach another coach's skaters. I tried to justify it by not charging you for sessions, but then I realized something. He can help us."

"How?" I took off my blade covers and hopped on the ice by leaping right over the barrier.

"He has a lot of clout with the US Figure Skating Association. He can easily get your pairs registration for the Las Vegas Invitational changed to individual." Marci had to yell so I could hear her as I started speed skating around the rink.

"The Las Vegas Invitational? Marci, that's less than a month away." I stopped in front of her and said, "I can't get a program together in that amount of time. I'm not ready."

"Yes, you are. And Renitsky agrees."

"You showed him our routine?"

She nodded excitedly.

The Las Vegas Invitational wasn't a huge competition or anything. It wasn't even a qualifier for the Olympics. Kimmy and I were just using it as an opportunity to try out a new routine. And now both Marci and Renitsky wanted me to use it to debut my solo career.

I had to admit I was a little excited by the prospect. Okay, I was a lot excited. When I started this routine with Marci, I thought it would be at least a year or so before I competed on my own. I thought Kimmy would be out of the hospital by then and able to cheer me on from the stands. That's when a wave of sadness washed over me. How could I do this without Kimmy? She still wasn't out of the woods yet. It was just too soon.

"This is a great opportunity," Marci said when I didn't respond. "You are going to burst onto the world stage. The publicity after people see you skate is going to be insane. I guarantee you are going to get sponsors just from this one performance. No more relying on your parents to support your skating."

I perked up at this prospect. The idea of doing something without my parents was definitely appealing. My desire to spend as little time as possible with my parents had only grown since their little fistfight in Kimmy's hospital room. Plus, the idea that Bria might be related to us just gnawed at my soul. One or possibly both of them had been lying to me for my entire life. Never mind the fact that their lies could cost me the woman I love forever, it could also cost Kimmy's life. If we had known that Bria and Kimbra were possibly related immediately, Bria could have donated so much sooner.

Ten days. We searched for a donor for ten days as Kimmy got weaker and weaker all the while not knowing that Bria could have saved her life. If Kimmy didn't make it, I didn't know if I would be able to forgive them for those ten days.

"I need to think about this," I said, skating away from her and into a double Salchow. I landed badly. I wasn't warm enough.

"Okay, fine," Marci said. "While you're thinking about it, why don't you run through what we have so far?"

I spent about thirty minutes warming up and then signaled to Marci to start the music. The routine she had created was so dynamic that I got a surge of energy and excitement just by hearing the opening notes of Gary Clark Jr.'s version of "Come Together" by The Beatles. It was an upbeat, pulsating rock anthem that couldn't help but draw people in. And between the music and Marci's choreography, I looked like a rock star while skating. She had me spinning and flying over the ice at dizzying speeds and somehow every major jump landed on a strong downbeat. I felt like a superhero. This routine was three minutes of pure magic.

When I struck my finishing pose, there was a spontaneous outburst of clapping and cheers from the Little League hockey team who were waiting to take the ice next.

"Mom, can I have figure skating lessons?" one of the boys asked.

Marci was screaming in excitement as she joined me on the ice. "That was amazing! Alexander, you are ready. You are so ready," she said.

"She's right," I heard Renitsky say from the stands. I looked up to see my pairs coach nodding in approval. That was so strange to me. Renitsky never gave his approval of a new routine until we had rehearsed it all the way through over one hundred times. He counted. He never even complimented Kimmy or me until he had seen the routine exactly one hundred times. So for him to say this, I knew Marci's choreography had to be impressive. "Of course, there are some transitions you need to clean up. And what is with your arms flailing about like a hunted turkey during that second Salchow?" Okay, there it was. There was the criticism I was used to. "But beyond that, you are more than ready for an Invitational."

"Don't believe us?" Marci said. "How about her?" She turned around her iPad to reveal Kimmy on the screen.

"You told her?" I asked Marci, immediately upset.

"Don't be mad at her, Xan," Kimmy said. "One of my friends told me you had been skating with her. I called her, not the other way around."

"You're not mad at me for not telling you?" I asked.

"I'm not but even if I was, after seeing that routine … I can't even … " Her mouth was agape as she stared at me with what looked like a mix of shock and confusion. "Xan, how did you ... I didn't know you could skate like that. You did a triple Lutz, stopped on a dime and changed direction. Sweet Cheez-Its! How is that even possible?"

I shrugged. "Great choreography, I guess."

Kimmy shook her head. "The choreography may be great but the execution, your execution, was precise and ... and gorgeous."

"Thanks, kid."

"No, thank you. Thanks for representing us in Las Vegas."

"I didn't actually agree to—"

"Oh, you're doing it."

"But what about you?"

"What about me? Watching you skate right now made me feel better than I have in a month. If you want me to keep feeling better you will shut up and do the damn thing!"

"Well, all right." I looked at Marci and said, "I guess I'm doing the damn thing."

Chapter 31: Xander

After rehearsal with Marci, I went home intending to spend as little time as possible there. I was just going to shower and then head to the hospital. But when I got home, I found my mother sitting alone at the kitchen table.

"Sit with me, Dmitri," she said in Russian.

I didn't want to, but something about the way she said it made me feel sorry for her. She didn't actually say Dimitri but a word in Russian that was hard to translate but was like, "little Dmitri love." She used to call me that when I was little. Back before I realized she wasn't a normal mom.

"Bria and her father are so much alike, it's a bit scary," my mom said once I sat down.

"What do you mean?"

"They are both methodical and literal and absolutely brilliant. And at first, they come across as so emotionless, right? But then when they show you even a glimpse of the emotion and … and passion within them that's brimming just below the surface, it feels like some sort of gift from the gods." She said all this in Russian. She was always much more expressive in her native tongue. And even though she worked hard to make sure Kimmy and I could speak the language so we would always be able to communicate with our grandparents, I had to admit my understanding wasn't perfect. I wasn't sure what she was trying to tell me.

"What do you mean?" I asked. "What kind of emotion?"

"I met him before I met your father, you know. He was so beautiful and smart. I never met anyone who spoke like him. He came into the bar where I was working one night. He'd just had a fight with his wife. She's an idiot, you know. She has no idea what she has in him."

"Oh God," I said as things started to become clear. "You loved him, didn't you?" My mother nodded. "You had an affair with him." It was more of a statement than a question. "Did Dad know?"

"He suspected a couple of years after Kimbra was born. That's why we stopped associating with the Browning family. He wanted to keep me as far away as possible from Jeffrey."

"Did he know? Did he know that Kimbra was Jeffrey Browning's daughter?"

My mother burst into tears. "No, he couldn't have known," she said while crying hysterically. "I didn't even know."

"You mean, in sixteen years you didn't have a clue?" I had no intention of comforting her or trying to calm her tears. I needed answers and I was not about to let her hysterics get her out of answering my questions.

Shaking her head frantically she said, "I didn't know. Before she was born, I knew it was possible. But when she was born she came out looking so white, I took it as a sign. I honestly thought she was Patrick's daughter. I thought it was a sign that I shouldn't leave him and that I should try to make my marriage work."

"I don't believe this." I stood up and walked around the kitchen. I was tempted to take a swig from the bottle of whiskey my mother was nursing but I resisted.

"We had an affair for five years, but it ended. I ended it. We never saw each other again. We had no contact with the Brownings until you started dating Bria."

"That was why Dad flipped out. It wasn't because she was black. It was because her dad had ... " I couldn't even bring myself to say it.

"When Kimmy got sick and Bria was a match, Jeffrey did a paternity test and we figured it out. Kimmy and Bria are half sisters."

"My God. Do you have any idea how complicated you have made my life?" I asked as I sat down again and put my head in my hands.

"Everything happens for a reason." My mother poured another glass of whiskey and pushed it toward me. Was she seriously giving me alcohol? "If it wasn't for this," she continued, "Bria wouldn't have been a match and Kimmy would have died."

"You can't be serious," I said. "Are you trying to say this is a good thing?"

"Well it's true," she said, finishing her drink and pouring another. She nodded toward the one she'd poured for me as if telling me it was okay for me to drink it.

Instead of taking her up on her offer, I yelled. "You cheated on Patrick!"

"As if he hasn't cheated on me time and time again."

"My sister and my girlfriend are sisters!"

"Okay, I admit, that is complicated," she said.

"My sister is related to the woman I love," I said, trying to make that piece of information seep into my head.

"Dmitri," she said, using the affectionate nickname again. "You are young, okay? You will love again, yes?" she said in English.

"No, not like this. I will never love anyone like I love Bria. You don't understand. How am I supposed to live with this?"

"It could be worse. She could be your sister as well. I mean, timing wise I was—"

"If you ever want me to look at you again, do not finish that sentence." I could guess what she was about to say. Probably something to the effect that Bria and I could easily be half brother and sister. Yes, that would definitely be worse. I took a deep breath and said, "Are you sure that I'm not…you know?" I wasn't even able to say it out loud.

My mother nodded. "Patrick ordered a paternity test before he would marry me." She sighed. "I wanted you to be Jeffrey's. I thought maybe if you were, he would leave his wife for me. I loved him so much." She wiped away a tear and then took another shot of whiskey.

My heart was beating so quickly I could barely breathe. I couldn't believe what she was telling me. One simple twist of fate, one day or week difference would have meant Bria and I were brother and sister. That thought pushed me over the edge. It was all the motivation I needed to take that drink she had poured. And then another.

Chapter 32: Bria

Gaganjyot took longer than expected to complete the test. He wanted to be sure of the results for me so he called his professor to go over everything as well. The hours drifted to dinner time and Gaganjyot offered to take me out.

"Thanks for coming with me," he said as we sat down to dinner at an Italian restaurant.

"Thanks for helping me with the DNA test stuff," I said. Then he just smiled at me. "What?"

"This is kind of like a date, right?" he asked hopefully.

"Gaganjyot, I have a boyfriend ... I think."

"You think? Look, Bria," he said. "You can talk to me, okay? What's going on?"

A lump developed in my throat. I didn't really want to talk to him about it, but I felt I needed to. "Do you remember Xander Vaughn?"

"Of course I do. He's the guy who snagged you away from me the last time. You guys together again?"

I nodded. "He, um, has a little sister."

"Yeah, the one with cancer. I saw it on the news."

"Aplastic anemia actually. She needed a bone marrow transplant which I provided."

"What? That's crazy. If you are a bone marrow match to his sister, then that would mean ... Oh. Oh. Wow," he said. "That's what the samples are? You and Xander?"

I nodded again.

We were silent for a while until a way too cheerful waiter came over to take our order, practically shoving the oyster appetizer down our throats. Who ordered oysters in Colorado?

"Well, it's possible," Gaganjyot began after the waiter left, "that it is just a coincidence." He could barely say it convincingly. I could tell he was just trying to make me feel better.

"You know better than I do how unlikely that is given that I'm black and she's white."

"Yeah, but isn't your dad half white? I mean genetics are a funny thing."

"Not that funny ... "

Just then, Gaganjyot's phone buzzed. As he looked at it, a smile crept across his face. He held it up to show me and said, "No match. You and Xander are not related. Ninety-five percent confidence."

I burst into tears. I cried so hard I could barely breathe. I started hyperventilating.

Gaganjyot came over to my side of the table and put his arm around me. "Come on, Bria. Breathe," he said, demonstrating the deep breaths he wanted me to take. After I could breathe again, he said, "I assume dinner is off?"

"I'm so sorry. I didn't mean to do this to you ... again. I just need to go see him."

He sighed. "It's okay," he said, scooting out of the booth to let me out. "Just promise you'll come visit me again, okay? Hey, bring a sample from Kimmy and I'll run it to see if you really are siblings."

I said I would, but honestly, I didn't care. As long as I hadn't been making out with my brother, I didn't care about anything else in the world.

Chapter 33: Xander

I drank too much. I didn't mean to, but I did. I wanted to drink away the thoughts of my mother with Bria's dad.

After too much whiskey, I passed out in the living room, still a little drunk but alert enough to drive when I woke up. I had to find Bria and tell her we weren't related. I also needed to tell Kimmy what our mother had told me. I finally took that shower I had been planning to take hours ago and I headed to the hospital.

I sat in the waiting room of the oncology ward trying to gather my emotions. I had planned on going straight up to Kimmy's room but I wasn't sure how or if to tell her about Bria. How did you tell someone they suddenly had a sister? Maybe I shouldn't tell her. Would it upset her more? Maybe I should let her parents tell her. No, it would be better coming from me.

I also had to take a moment to breathe a sigh of relief that I wasn't related to Bria. Sure, I would have to deal with the fact that her sister was my sister but since we weren't directly related, I might be able to live with it. Of course, there was the possibility that my mother was still lying. She had been lying for years already; who's to say she didn't just tell me what I wanted to hear?

After closing my eyes and taking a couple of deep breaths, I had just decided to head to Kimmy's room when

I opened my eyes and saw Bria standing in front of me. Tears were streaming down her face and she was shaking.

"Bria? Are you okay?" I said, standing.

Shaking her head she said, "We're not related," as she dropped her crutches and leaped into my arms.

"I know. I know." I held her tightly as she cried. "I love you," I said into her hair.

"I love you, so much, Xander."

"I'm never gonna let you go," I added. "It's you and me forever, okay?"

She nodded into my chest.

We stood there in an embrace for so long that people started to stare. I didn't mind though. The oncology waiting room was often the scene for emotional embraces. I was glad to be able to provide a happy embrace.

"Wait," Bria said suddenly as she pulled away. "How did you find out we weren't related? I had a DNA test and I just got the results."

I sighed and said, "I had a long conversation with my mother and I found out everything."

"Everything?"

I took Bria's hand and led her to a place that was more secluded. She was still limping so it took a little while to get to the empty stairwell. "You were right," I said once we were away from the possibly perked ears of strangers. "My mom and your dad ... they had an affair. You and Kimmy are sisters."

"I have a sister," she said to herself. It was a bittersweet moment. Bria had always wanted a sibling. She hated being alone. She hated having no one that understood what she was going through living with two parents that ignored her. But now that she finally had a sister, that sister just so happened to be the sister of the man she loved. "This is insane," she said, hugging herself as if she were cold.

"I know," I said. "But we can get past this, right? It's not too insane, is it?" I asked hopefully.

Bria kissed me deeply but then suddenly pulled away.

"You've been drinking," she said.

"I … Why … Not really. I mean, just a little."

"How much?" she asked as she stepped away from me.

"Just four … maybe six shots. I don't … I lost count."

Bria closed her eyes and shook her head. "You had six shots, probably more, and then drove here?"

"Bria, I'm not drunk. I just had a few drinks. I was stressed out after talking to my mother."

She didn't say anything for several minutes. I could practically see her mind at work probably calculating my blood alcohol level.

"I don't see why this is such a big deal," I said finally.

"I can't handle this right now," she said. "Let's just go talk to Kimmy."

She tried to walk past me but I grabbed her arm. "Let's talk about this now. What's going on?"

Bria took a deep breath then said, "Do you remember how you felt when I was in a coma and you didn't know if I would make it or not?"

"Of course, I do. I never want—"

"Well, I've felt that way before, too. About you."

"What are you talking about?" I asked, completely confused. When had I ever been close to death?

"June 17. Two months after we broke up."

"I don't have a color-coded calendar in my head, Bria. I have no idea what happened on that date," I said with a smile. She didn't find it funny.

"Kimmy called me for help in the middle of the night. Both of you had been drinking too much to make it home on your own. When I found you, you were passed out, barely breathing and unresponsive."

Suddenly, it all became clear. "Mitchell Clark's party. You got me home that night."

Bria nodded. "Xander, we have been through so much. So much more than two people our age should ever have to go through. And it has made us stronger. But not that strong. I'm not strong enough to lose you."

"Why would you lose me?"

"Because you have alcoholic tendencies. And you have six drinks and then drive."

"You think I'm an alcoholic?" I asked, fighting the urge to get offended.

"Did I say that? No. I said you have alcoholic tendencies." She took a step closer to me and then rested her head on my chest. "I love you, Xander. You know I do. And because I love you, please don't be hurt when I tell you that you have more of your parents in you than you care to admit."

My immediate reaction was to get angry, but I held back. She was right. I did have alcoholic tendencies not to mention anger issues, just like my father.

"You're right," I said, wrapping my arms around her. "I'm sorry I scared you that night. I'm sorry for making you worry."

"Really?" she asked looking up at me. "You're not mad at me?"

"For what? Caring enough about me to tell me the truth?" I shook my head. "That's what you do when you love someone." Saying that out loud made me realize just how screwed up my parents had made me. It also made me realize how thankful I was to Bria for showing me what a real loving relationship was supposed to look and feel like.

Kimmy was asleep when we arrived at her room and we didn't want to wake her. Instead, Bria and I cuddled in the recliner together, alternating between staring into each other's eyes as if we had never seen them before, intertwining our fingers, and brushing our lips together.

"Well, I take it you're back together," Kimmy said suddenly.

Bria hopped off my lap as if she were embarrassed to be caught showing me affection.

" 'Bout time you woke up, lazy bum." I stood up and went over to her bed. "We have something to tell you," I said after kissing her forehead.

Bria and I stared at each other awkwardly, each of us trying to decide who should speak first. Finally, she said, "I had a DNA test done."

Then I added, "And I talked to Mom."

"And?" Kimmy asked when neither one of us volunteered any further information.

"We're sisters!" Bria blurted.

Kimmy didn't look as surprised as I thought she would. I think she had already figured it out.

"And you and Xan?" she asked.

"We're not related," I volunteered. "Mom and Bria's dad are your parents. Mom and Patrick are my parents."

"Wow," was all Kimmy said. She stared straight down at the bed as if thinking about what to say next.

"I know it's a lot to take—"

"I've always wanted a sister," Kimmy said interrupting me.

"Me too!" Bria hugged Kimmy tightly.

"Hey, Xan, do you think you can do me a favor?" Kimmy asked.

"Yeah, sure, anything."

"I need a moment alone with my sister." She smiled. Well, she tried to smile. The joy was not in her eyes. "Girl talk," she added reassuringly.

Before leaving the room, I kissed both of them on the top of the head. They were both my girls. We were somehow going to create a new type of family, just the three of us. It was going to be great. I could feel it.

Nearly an hour later, Bria walked out of the room, eyes wide.

"You okay?" I asked her.

"Yeah, yeah, fine."

"How's Kimmy? What did you talk about?"

Bria took a deep breath and said, "She's fine. She went back to sleep."

"What did you talk about?" I asked again.

"I can't answer that. I made her a promise, so please don't ask again." Something about her tone of voice made me take the request very seriously. If it was some sort of special sister bond, I didn't want to infringe on that. Instead, I tried to change the mood. "What now?" I asked, wrapping my arms around her waist and pulling her close to me.

"Can I watch you skate?" she asked.

"Right now?" I took out my phone and looked at the time. It was almost three o'clock in the morning.

Bria nodded. "Call and see if they will open the rink for you. I haven't seen you skate in weeks. I miss it."

"Okay, let's go."

Chapter 34: Xander

Before going to the rink that morning, we went to Denny's and talked about our situation. We were committed to each other, there was no question about that. But there were so many questions about other things. What in the world was going on with our parents? We needed answers. And Bria had a plan to get them. She wanted to confront all four of our parents all together. And the very next day, that was exactly what she did.

"What are you doing here?" Annette Browning asked her husband as she entered Mrs. Schnauzer's office.

"I got a call from the guidance counselor saying there was a problem with Bria's paperwork for college," Jeffrey Browning said. "She said I needed to come in and sign some forms."

"She told me Bria was pregnant," Annette Browning said.

"I'm sorry," Mrs. Schnauzer said. "Both of those were lies."

Suddenly my mom and dad came in as well.

"What is this?" Patrick said. "Some sort of intervention?"

"You said Dmitri had a broken leg," my mom said to Mrs. Schnauzer.

"Yeah, also lies," Mrs. Schnauzer said. "I'm sorry, this is so unprofessional, but we really needed to get all of you here today."

"Why?" Annette Browning said. "There is no point to this. I don't want to hear anything these people have to say."

"What about what we have to say?" Bria said, standing.

"How about the four of you stop being selfish pricks and listen to what your children need for once?" I added.

The parents stared at each other awkwardly for a moment then one by one, took a seat.

"Fine, what do you want?" Mr. Browning asked.

"We just need answers," Bria said. "We've figured out a lot of things on our own."

"Like the fact that Bria and Kimbra are half sisters," I interrupted.

Mr. Browning and my mom looked down guiltily. Mrs. Browning pursed her lips angrily and looked away while my father balled his hands in to fists.

"But we need some blanks filled in," Bria continued.

"I don't have time for this," Patrick said as he headed for the door.

"You are a retired mediocre hockey player. You have plenty of time for this. Sit your ass down and listen to what we have to say." I didn't mean to come off sounding so aggressive, but I was fed up.

My dad stared at me for a second with something that looked a little like respect. He took a seat and both our moms followed.

"Whether you like it or not," Bria began, "the Vaughns and the Brownings are forever connected. Whether it's through Kimmy or through the marriage of Xander and me." Bria grabbed my hand.

"You got married?" my mother yelled.

"Please say you didn't get married," Bria's mom said, putting her head in her hands.

"No, we didn't get married," Bria said. "But we are. And soon."

"We are?" I said, looking at her. We hadn't discussed that part. Not that I was complaining. I was just surprised. She smiled and nodded. "Yeah, we are," I said with more conviction.

"Given our connection, you all have to decide right here and now, are we going to bring everything out in the open and try to forgive and be a family or are we going to keep up the lies, the stonewalling, and the complete disconnect? Are we going to keep ignoring each other? 'Cause Xander and I will disappear and you will never see your grandchildren."

"Dear God, you *are* pregnant!" Annette Browning cried.

"No, Mom, I'm not pregnant!" Bria said exasperated. "Is that all you care about? You don't want to be a grandmother too soon?"

"That's not why I'm upset." Annette Browning stood and then sat down again. "Getting pregnant with you," she began, "it changed something in me and unfortunately it wasn't for the best."

"What are you talking about?" Bria asked.

"Postpartum depression," Bria's dad volunteered. "Your mother could barely function after you were born. She was nearly catatonic. Needless to say, it put a strain on our relationship."

"So, you thought it was a good idea to cheat on your sick wife who just had a baby?" Bria asked.

"It just happened. We didn't plan it," Jeffrey said. "It was a moment of weakness."

The room fell silent.

"You're lying," I said finally. All four of the parents looked up at me. "My mother already told me that it was possible that I could have been Jeffrey's son as well. Which means the affair started long before Bria and I were born and didn't end until Bria and I were four."

Silence again.

"What are you not telling us?" I asked.

More silence.

"About five years?" Annette Browning said suddenly. "Nadia has you believing their affair only lasted five years."

I looked at my mom and Jeffrey. Neither of them would return my gaze. Even my dad was uncharacteristically quiet and noncombative.

"I only got pregnant to try to save my marriage," Annette continued.

I felt Bria's hand grow cold in mine. It was as if all the life and blood was draining out of her body. For a second, it reminded me of the way Kimmy's hand felt that day on the ice when she fainted. When I squeezed her hand, she turned and gave me a look that said 'I'm okay.'

"The baby didn't help," Annette said. "It made things worse. Nothing could keep Jeffrey and Nadia apart. And I do mean nothing. Which is why, twenty years later, they're still together."

"Hold up," Bria said suddenly animated. "I'm gonna temporarily ignore the fact that you just called me an 'it' and focus on the twenty-year affair. Dad, you've been cheating on Mom for twenty years?"

"That can't be true," I said, looking at my parents for some sort of reassurance. Neither of them would look at me."

"Wednesday night book club?" Annette said in reference to my mom's weekly ritual. "Have you ever seen your Russian whore of a mother even touch a book?"

"Hey, hey, hey! Let's not resort to name calling," Mrs. Schnauzer said, trying to reign in the conversation.

"Wednesday is their date night. Has been for twenty years," Bria's mom continued.

"This is insane!" I yelled. "Why didn't you people just get a divorce?"

"Because I didn't know," Patrick said. "I caught them kissing once when you were four. Your mom said it was just a kiss. I forbid her from seeing the Browning family again. We switched pediatricians. I didn't allow you and Bria to play together anymore. I thought that was the end of it until Kimmy got sick. When Bria turned out to be a match ... I figured out there was more to the story. Then Annette told me everything."

"And you, Mom?" Bria asked. "Why didn't you divorce him?"

"Because he shouldn't get off that easy!" Annette yelled, standing. "Why should he get off scot-free and leave me to take care of ... "

"Take care of what?" Bria offered. "A child you didn't want? An inconvenient 'it'?"

"I didn't say that," Annette said.

"You stayed to make him miserable and ended up making me miserable in the process as well," Bria said. "I'm just a casualty of your selfish, pathetic, destructive lives."

A somber silence fell over the room again as Annette sat down and collected her emotions.

"Well, we haven't heard anything from the happy couple in a while," I said in reference to my mom and Jeffrey. "What do you two have to say for yourselves?"

"We really didn't mean for any of this to happen. We didn't mean to hurt anyone," Jeffrey said.

"Really?" Bria said sarcastically. "You thought having a twenty-year extramarital affair would somehow work out well?"

"You shouldn't talk to him like that," Nadia chimed in. "He is a good man who did a bad thing."

"Lady, there are 1,040 Wednesdays in twenty years. I'd say he did a lot of bad things," Bria said.

"That's it. I'm done," my father said, standing and heading to the door.

"Patrick. Dad, wait," I said, feeling sorry for him for the first time. It couldn't have been easy finding out your wife had been sleeping with another man for twenty years. And even without him knowing the full truth, there had to have been an undercurrent of resentment during their entire strained marriage. "We still have things to figure out. For Kimmy's sake," I said.

"Have her real father take care of her," he said before exiting the office and slamming the door behind him.

"Patrick!" I yelled, going after him.

Bria grabbed my arm and pulled me back to her. "No, let him go," she said. "In fact, you all can go. You're all broken, horrible people and there's no fixing you. Even if there were a way to fix you, that's not our job. We are your children! You're supposed to be taking care of us. So you know what? Just go. Go cheat on each other for another twenty years for all I care. Xander, Kimmy and I will start our own little family without you."

"And it will be more normal than anything any of you have ever provided," I added.

Chapter 35: Bria

I was furious as I left Mrs. Schnauzer's office. I wasn't even sure who I was more angry at. Of course, the obvious choice was my dad and Xander's mom. They were the ones having the twenty-year affair. But then there was also my mom. How selfish was it to stay in a loveless marriage just to make the other person miserable? Wouldn't the loving thing to do be to make a life that was better for me, her only daughter? But no, she never even considered my feelings, just her own righteous anger.

Oddly enough, the person who was least to blame was Xander's dad, Patrick. He was clueless about the affair. But then again, he did just ultimately abandon Kimmy, the girl he thought was his daughter for the past sixteen years. How do you do that? Yeah, there was nothing redeemable about any of our parents.

We didn't need them. Now, it was our turn. Xander, Kimmy and I were going to be a family. I had been delaying thinking about the future for a while because I was afraid. I didn't know what was going to happen with Kimmy, I hadn't chosen a college, and I didn't know where Xander's career was headed. But that was about to change. Graduation was less than a month away. Xander's solo debut in Las Vegas was just over a week away. And according to Marci Wong, his debut was going to be life changing. It would put his career on the fast-track to the Olympics. Thus, it was time to make some decisions.

While Xander went to the hospital, I went to Staples and loaded up on supplies. Then I checked into a hotel. There was no way I was going back to my parents' house. I was done with them. Perhaps forever. Maybe I would send Xander to pack up a few of my things, but if I never saw them again, I'd not only survive, I'd probably thrive.

Six hours later, my research was complete. Now all I needed to do was show Xander.

When I opened the door to my hotel room, Xander started kissing me before I could even say anything. "Whoa, Xan, hold up," I said. "I want to show you my research."

"Your what?"

"My research. Look at all the planning I did for our future." I spun around the hotel room, showing him all the giant Post-it notes affixed to the walls.

"Oh, research," he said, disappointed.

"What did you think I wanted?"

Xander held up his phone and said, "Bria, it's one o'clock in the morning. You texted 'I need you' and then a hotel and room number. What did you think I would think?"

"Oh, oh. I didn't even think of that. Sorry." And then inexplicably, I started laughing.

"Are you laughing at me?" he asked. "Dude, that is cold."

"I'm not laughing at you. But you have to admit it's kind of funny. Did you think this was some sort of Lifetime movie?" I laughed harder. "I'm sorry. I'm so sorry. We can ... you know ... if you want to."

"No, it's weird now. Let me see your research."

"Each Post-it note represents a college that I was accepted to," I said when I was finally able to stop laughing. And there's two extra for University of Denver and Community College of Denver which I didn't apply to but I'm pretty sure I could get in. Now, since this isn't all about me, I also have factored in your skating career and Kimmy's health. So each Post-it has where you could potentially skate as well as possible coaches. For Kimmy, I have listed possible health care providers in case she has a relapse. Since we were only a haploid match, we have to make sure she is nearby a facility that can use the same technique for a transplant in case she needs another donation from me."

"Sweet Cheez-Its," Xander said. "You did all this today?"

"Yes, but there's more. Each Post-it has a numerical score based on a rating system I created. There is a number for you, for me, and for Kimmy based on what is most advantageous on a scale of one to ten. For example." I grabbed one of my crutches and hobbled to the other side of the room where the Post-it for Duke was located and said, "Duke is a nine for me but it is a three for you based on the caliber of coaches I could find in that area."

"Which school wins based on your analysis?" Xander was grinning but I couldn't tell whether he was pleased or just thought I was a nutcase.

"It's not that simple. I also had to factor in living expenses. So I created an elimination system before moving on to that stage. Any of the nineteen schools that scored below a twenty out of thirty for our combined best interests was eliminated. That left seven schools. They move on to the next round which takes place on this wall."

Xander studied the choices for a moment. "Wait a minute. How in the world did the two Denver schools make the list? Those are not in your best interests."

"That's just it, Xander. They may not be in my best interests but it's not all about me anymore. We are a family now and I have to think about you and Kimmy. Staying here is best for you because you would get to keep working with Marci Wong and it's closer to Dr. Givens for Kimmy. Even though they only get a two from me, that was enough to get them a score of twenty-two and into the next round."

Xander never took his eyes off of me during my whole spiel. "We are a family now," he said, weaving our fingers together. "What's next?"

"Okay, so for these seven schools, I researched living expenses for the cities, housing, and jobs you and I can take on."

"Bria, you're planning on working *and* going to school?"

"Of course! Do you have any idea how expensive skating is? Even if Kimmy stays on your parents' insurance, and I have a free ride to school and you get sponsorships for your skates and rink time, we will be cutting it close even if both of us work."

"Wow, Bria, this is scary."

"Um, yeah, it is. But we don't have a choice. If we want to be together and away from our parents, this is the way it has to be. We can do it, Xan. I believe in us."

Tears welled in his eyes. "Just when I think I can't love you more, I do."

"I love you, too." Xander leaned in to kiss me when there was a knock on the door. We simultaneously looked at the clock on the nightstand. Who would be knocking on my hotel room at this time of the night? Who even knew where I was? I surely didn't tell my parents. Of course, since my dad paid my credit card bill, he could have easily just looked at my recent charges and figured out where I was. But when Xander opened the door, it wasn't my dad. It was his.

"How did you know I was here?" Xander asked.

"I tracked your phone," Mr. Vaughn said.

"Yeah, of course you did." Xander threw his hands up in the air in frustration. "God, I'll be so happy when I'm out from under your thumb. I can't take this anymore."

"Look, I didn't come here to fight with you, son."

"Yeah, then why did you come here?"

"I want to apologize to you and to Bria," he said.

Xander was stunned into silence and immobility. He hadn't even opened the door all the way.

"Do you want to come in, Mr. Vaughn?" I asked, pushing Xander out of the way with my crutch and letting Mr. Vaughn enter.

After entering the room, Mr. Vaughn rubbed his scruffy beard as if he were uncomfortable and agitated. "I, um, haven't been the best father to say the least," he began. "I think I took out my frustrations with my life on you and, um, I shouldn't have done that."

Xander nodded slowly but didn't respond.

"Sure, I didn't know your mother was cheating on me but that was probably because I didn't *want* to know. And, honestly, I can't say that I was completely innocent during our marriage either. I failed as a husband and I failed as a father and I hope you just don't follow my example."

A silence followed that I wasn't sure if I should fill or not. This seemed like an important father son moment and I didn't want to interfere. Thankfully, Mr. Vaughn kept talking.

"We're getting a divorce, by the way. I went to see a lawyer today. I know this is bad timing with Kimmy being in the hospital and all, but is there ever a good time to get a divorce?" He chuckled, trying to lighten the mood. It didn't work. "What's all this?" he asked, pointing to my Post-It notes.

"Bria is working on a plan for our future. She's figuring out a way for all of us to be together while she goes to college, I continue skating, and Kimmy gets the medical assistance she needs."

Mr. Vaughn nodded as he studied the top seven choices. "Why are you even considering a community college?" he asked. "Didn't you get into all of the Ivy League schools?"

"Yeah, but with living expenses it will be cheaper for us to stay close to here," I said.

Mr. Vaughn kept reading the Post-Its, stopping on the one for University of Pennsylvania. "Hey, Xan, remember when you were twelve and I played for the Philadelphia Flyers for a season?"

"Yeah, I remember," Xander said. "You were gone more often than usual."

"That was because I actually bought a house there. It's about fifteen minutes away from the University of Pennsylvania." He looked at us and said, "It's yours if you want it."

"Why do you still have a house you haven't lived in for six years? Who has been in it?" Xander asked.

"Do you really want me to answer that?" he said.

"Never mind," Xander answered. I assumed he had kept the house for a mistress or something. "The person who was living there moved out last month. I was going to sell it, but I would rather give it to you and your girlfriend."

"You want to give us a house? Free and clear?" Xander asked.

He shrugged. "Why not? You could even rent out the basement and make some income."

"Are you serious?" I asked.

"Totally," he said.

"Xander, with a place to live, plus money coming in, we can do it. We can make this work."

As if not able to believe his father's change of heart, Xander asked, "Why are you doing this?"

"You're all I have left," he said.

Chapter 36: Bria

The next four months went by like a blur. Xander, of course, dominated the Las Vegas Invitational. Sponsors were lining up to sign him for endorsement deals. There was actually a bidding war. We wouldn't need to worry about his skates, costumes, or rink time for years. That still meant we had to pay for coaching but having the basics covered would be huge for us.

After a ton of help from Xander and Kimmy, I was able to give the valedictorian speech. In the end, I actually did just visualize that everyone in the audience was Heidi Hopley.

All of our parents came to graduation. None of them sat together. It was weird, awkward and painful, and, honestly, I wished they hadn't shown up at all. My stubborn ass parents still didn't get a divorce. My dad did move in with Nadia and apparently, as long as my mom kept the house and the Bentley, she was fine with that. I, however, was not comfortable with the idea that my father was living with my husband's mother and I wanted to get as far away from them as possible. Oh yeah, Xander and I got married at the first possible opportunity, which happened to be in Las Vegas during the debut of his solo skating career. And I am happy to report that there was no Rihanna involved. I probably should have led with the whole marriage bit of information. I kind of buried the lead there.

Anyway, Nadia, of course, wanted Kimmy to live with her and Jeffrey when she was better, but Kimmy adamantly refused. And since you can't really argue with someone who just beat a complete acute aplasia it was easily decided that she would move in with Xander and me.

Right after graduation, Kimmy was released from the hospital. Instead of going to my summer research program at Stanford, I spent the summer taking care of her so Xander could train. He didn't want me to give up such a prestigious opportunity, but that's what family does. I had a new theory about family. A family was what you made it. A family made sacrifices for each other. At least, that's what our family would do. We were going to try our best to be nothing like our parents. We were a new kind of family.

The house that Xander's dad gave us was perfect and just what we needed. It had three bedrooms upstairs and a finished basement which Xander was able to fix up and rent out almost immediately.

Things were tight, but we made it work. And every time an emergency came up, I used my credit card and it never failed. My dad kept paying it for me. That was the way he showed his love for me. That was all he was capable of and I had to accept that.

Something had always bothered me about when Xander and I broke up the first time. We knew it was Kimmy who sent the text to me from Xander's phone, but we never did quite figure out who sent the letter to him on my stationery. That was until I got a letter in the mail one day from my dad. In the envelope was a check for ten thousand dollars as well as a typed note written on my stationery that simply said, "I'm sorry." That was my dad's way of admitting he had sent the note while apologizing as well. Was he trying to bribe me for his forgiveness? Too bad. I would never forgive him. But I was totally going to cash that check.

By the time my classes started at University of Pennsylvania, Kimmy was well enough to stay at home on her own or go with Xander to the rink. She wasn't strong enough to get back to skating on her own, but watching her brother was enough to satisfy her for the time being. Kimmy kept herself busy by obsessively planning Xander's future and arranging anything she could to help him get chosen for the Olympic team.

That part of skating was odd to me. I thought the selection of the team would be based on something more concrete like the scores from the qualifying competitions but apparently the selection was more subjective than that. Even if a person had the high score at Nationals, there was no guarantee that they would be selected for the team. To make sure this didn't happen, Kimmy basically became Xander's personal public relations firm. Using social media, she made sure Xander was the most popular figure skater in the country. There was no way the association could ignore him.

And it worked. He made the team.

Chapter 37: Xander

Over the next three years, Kimmy needed four more donations from Bria, which she willingly gave. Thankfully, Bria didn't have to suffer through any more staph infections. The first one left her with a permanent disability. Eventually, she would need a complete hip replacement. But for now, she made do with weekly physical therapy.

No one could explain why Kimmy's bone marrow kept failing, but it did. I felt so powerless whenever they were both in the hospital. But I think Bria felt even worse. She didn't know why her stem cells weren't enough to cure Kimmy.

Both of them had to miss several of my competitions over the years due to illness so when I was selected for the Olympic team, we decided as a family that Bria just had to go with me no matter what. And since Kim was in the middle of another relapse, that meant we had to call my mom and Bria's dad to come take care of her while we went to Beijing.

I hated leaving her. So did Bria. But what were we supposed to do? This was the Olympics. This was what our family had been fighting for together for the past three years. So while we were there, we called Kimmy every ten hours and gave her updates and play by plays of our time in Beijing.

"How are you feeling?" Marci Wong asked while I waited in the wings before my final free skate.

"Pretty good actually," I said, kind of shocked at how at ease I felt.

"Really?" Marci said. "I was freaking out at my first Olympics. I was so nervous I was shaking."

I shrugged. "Bria has a theory about that. Since this is my first Olympics, expectations for my success are pretty low. Even if I fall flat on my face, I can just chalk it up to inexperience and I get the sympathy of a nation. And if I succeed and medal, well, I'm a flat-out hero. It's a win-win so no pressure."

Marci nodded. "Smart girl."

"She really is." I looked around for a second. "Where is she, by the way?"

"Probably giving a TED Talk in Chinese or something," Marci said sarcastically. "I swear that girl's Mandarin is better than mine and my parents were born here."

I smiled. "My wife is amazing."

"Okay, okay, let's focus," Marci said. "You're in fourth place right now and only one more person after you. You are in perfect position for medaling. Skate a clean routine and you've got it."

I skated better than a clean program. It was a dream program. Marci had choreographed a routine to an a cappella version of Litost by X Ambassadors. It was the complete opposite of my short program to the Gary Clark Jr. song which was a fast-paced thrill ride that often got the crowd clapping along to the beat. My free skate was to a slow, soul stirring song with no music which often meant at times I was skating in pure silence. Marci thought the effect of me silently flying through the air would leave a powerful and indelible mark on the audience's minds. She was right. Every time I skated this routine over the past year, I'd see people wiping away tears when I finished. Which was why I didn't think anything of it when I saw tears streaming down Bria's face when I stepped off the ice.

She hugged me tightly.

"What are you doing back here?" I asked. They usually only let coaches in the "Kiss and Cry" area where you sit and find out your scores.

"Just ... I just ... " She wiped her tears away and said, "I love you. Go get your scores and meet me in the wings, okay?" She kissed me and walked away.

It wasn't until I sat down next to Marci in the "Kiss and Cry" that I realized something must be wrong.

Chapter 38: Bria

"What happened?" Xander asked me. The second his scores had been read, he jumped out of his seat and found me in the wings.

"You just won a gold medal," I said. "That's what happened." I smiled broadly, trying to convey the enthusiasm this moment deserved. Maybe that way I could delay telling him what I knew.

"What?" he asked, visibly confused. "There's still another skater. What are you talking about?"

"Xander. Sweetie. Did you pay any attention to what you scored? It is mathematically impossible for Manuel Baliaga to beat you. You just won a gold medal in the Olympics."

He didn't react the way I expected. He tilted his head to the side and said, "Really?"

"Yes, really. Are you doubting my math? Why are you not more excited?"

"Because I know something is wrong," he said.

I couldn't hide it from him. He knew me too well. I sighed. "I have something to show you," I said with a shaky voice, trying to keep myself from bursting into uncontrollable tears. I took his hand and led him to one of the warm-up rooms. Once he was seated, I took out my phone, cued up the video and hit play.

"Hi Xan," Kimmy's voice said. It was an old video from three years ago. Xander probably recognized it immediately from the hospital background and Kimmy's lack of hair. "I just want to let you know that you are my best friend and the best brother a girl could have. You are better than I deserve after what I did to break up you and Bria. I told her what I did, by the way, and she forgave me. I didn't want to leave ... " She paused as her voice started quivering. Instead of finishing that thought, she put on a smile and continued on a different track.

"If you're watching this, it means you won a gold medal and I'm not there ... for some reason. I am so proud of you. You really have no idea how proud I am. And I know you might think I would be jealous or something. But if I can't skate anymore then I am more than happy to have you skate for me. You would never admit it, but you're better than me. You have always been better than me. Alexander Vaughn, you were born to skate.

"Anyway, enjoy your gold medal and know that I am enjoying it with you. You're the best, Xan!"

There was a pause in the video and then a new, more recent recording began.

"Well, I'm sick again," Kimmy said. "I'm sick again and the Olympics are coming up. You made the team so I know your gold medal is coming. In fact, if you're watching this, you won. Congrats! Though, even if you won silver or bronze, I told Bria to let you watch anyway. But I'm pretty sure you won gold. I've seen your routines. They are breathtaking. Truly breathtaking, Xan. I have spent the past week watching videos of all the male figure skaters going against you and they don't have a chance against you. Seriously, you got this. I love you very much. I'll love you always."

The video cut out and then another recording began. "You and Bria are leaving for Beijing tomorrow and I want to say goodbye. Like for real goodbye." Kimmy closed her eyes but tears still slipped through. "I tried to fight for so long. But after four relapses in three years, I'm tired. I'm so tired. I held on for you, Xan. I thought I owed it to you. First, I broke you and Bria up and then because I got sick you found out that you and her might be related and that our parents are asshats. You have no idea how relieved I was when I found out you weren't brother and sister, and that you two could actually find a way to have a life together without burden or guilt weighing on you. I think the knowledge that you would always have Bria made this a little easier.

"I'm gonna die soon, Xan. In fact, I'm probably dead already. I made Bria promise that she wouldn't show you any of these videos until after I was gone. And now that I'm gone, I must insist that you skate, Xan. You have to keep skating even without me. It makes you so happy you don't even realize. It makes you almost as happy as Bria does. God, if you knew how your eyes light up just when someone says her name or the goofy grin you get when she walks into the room you'd be so embarrassed." Kimmy paused and giggled a bit.

"Anyway, if you have those two things, skating and Bria, I think you will be okay. I couldn't go without knowing you would be okay. And I have to go, Xan. I have to. I'm so tired.

"Please don't be sad ... Well, be a little sad. I mean I'm amazing and I won't be around anymore, but don't be sad forever, okay? Know that anytime you are on the ice, I am with you.

"I love you and I love my sister, Bria. She is everything that is good and right in the world. Take care of her and let her take care of you. And um, yeah, go win me a few more gold medals, will 'ya?"

"When did she record this?" he asked.

"The first part was right after she found out we were sisters three years ago," Bria said. "It was the hardest thing I ever had to do. I didn't want to lie to you."

"You didn't lie to me," he said, trying to reassure me. "You were keeping a promise to my ... our sister."

"Still I—"

"Is she ... is she gone?" he asked.

I nodded. "Our parents called. She died two hours ago."

Xander crumpled to the floor and heaved as if he were going to vomit. "I'm so sorry," I said as I held him and cried with him.

"She died without us? She was without her family," he cried. "I abandoned her. All for a stupid medal."

"No, Xander, this is not on you," I said. "This was the way she wanted it. She didn't want you there. She wanted you here doing what you love. Doing what she could no longer do. Kimmy had it all arranged, okay? She wanted you distracted. She wanted you skating. She didn't want you dwelling on her death."

"But what do I do now? What am I supposed to do without her?"

"We're going to figure that out together, okay?" I continued to hold him for a moment and when I could speak without my voice wavering, I said, "There are more."

"More what?"

"Recordings," I said. "She recorded a message for you for every life event she thought she might miss. It started three years ago and we've been updating them pretty regularly."

"How many more?" he asked, looking at me with such hope in his eyes.

"Sixteen."

"Sixteen? She made me sixteen recordings? What are they for? When do I see them?"

I shook my head. "I promised I wouldn't tell you. She didn't want to influence your life. She doesn't want you trying to accomplish something just because you think you'll get to watch a recording of her. If I told you there was one for after you climbed Everest, you'd climb Everest, wouldn't you?"

Xander wiped away tears and smiled. "Yeah, that's fair."

"You're just gonna have to trust me. Live your life. And when you least expect it, she'll be there waiting for you again. Because she's our family and family is always there for you."

###

Author's Note

Thank you for taking the time to read *Matchless*. As an independent author, the most effective way to promote my book is through word of mouth. So if enjoyed my work, please tell a friend and consider leaving a review. Thanks!